SNIFFING OUT SWEET SECRETS

A FAIRMONT FINDS CANINE COZY MYSTERY

CATE LAWLEY

ALSO BY CATE LAWLEY

FAIRMONT FINDS CANINE COZY MYSTERIES

On the Trail of a Killer (previously Fairmont Finds a Body)

The Scent of a Poet's Past (previously Fairmont Finds a Poet)

Sniffing Out Sweet Secrets (previously Fairmont Finds a Baker)

Tracking a Poison Pen

LOVE EVER AFTER

Heartache in Heels

Skeptic in a Skirt

Pretty in Peep-Toes

Love Ever After Boxed Set One

LUCKY MAGIC

Lucky Magic

Luck of the Devil

Luck of the Draw

Wicked Bad Luck

For the most current listing of Cate's books, visit her website:

www.CateLawley.com

For Vegas

PROLOGUE

My days are filled with teasing, chattering squirrels, naps in the sunshine, and bits of hand-fed treats.

They are also filled with my lady, Zella's, love.

I am the center of her world, and she is mine.

I am happy.

I am loved.

I only miss the hunt a little.

1

Some days can only be improved by deep-fried dough.

Or creamy icing atop deliciously moist cake.

This was one of those days. And since Helen was my best friend in White Sage, she'd offered up herself on the sacrificial altar of empty calories and a prolonged sugar high and agreed to accompany me at this ridiculously early hour.

It didn't hurt that she could eat like a teenage boy and not gain weight, but I knew she was here for me and not the baked goods. Well, she was here mostly for me.

Catie's Cupcakery didn't officially open until nine, but everyone knew that Catie started baking as early as five and never later than five thirty. At six thirty, she was guaranteed to not only be there, but also to have at least a few batches out of the oven, cooling, waiting for icing.

"Oh my," Helen muttered from the passenger seat of my Grand Cherokee.

I knew that tone. That was the tone my dear friend assumed when she recognized an impending event of some importance. I hesitated to use the word "crisis."

I was typically good in a crisis. I'd raised two children, and during that time had encountered my fair share of them.

But I wasn't up to it.

Not today.

We were approaching Sally's Sandwich Shoppe, just two stores from our end destination, Catie's Cupcakery.

I didn't have time for a crisis. Not that the world revolved around my needs...but it was a nice thought for a few seconds.

I'd just pulled even with Sally's storefront when Helen yelled, "Stop!"

Not stopping when a passenger you trust demands it would be foolish. I'd used up most of my allowance for foolish when I'd lingered overlong in a failing marriage, so I stopped as soon as I knew we wouldn't be rear-ended.

"Back up. We need to turn down Bluebonnet Lane."

Bluebonnet Lane was a small side street that led to a neighborhood but also to the Cupcakery's rear parking. I'd passed Bluebonnet without slowing, because I preferred the storefront parking at Sally's and Catie's over their shared parking in the rear.

"Is your back bothering you?" Because back pain was a very good reason Helen would want to turn down Bluebonnet Lane. The back entrance of Catie's shop had no steps, unlike the front.

She made a disgusted sound, as if the very thought that she'd be laid low by something so trivial was unthinkable. "Just back up and turn."

Instead of checking my rearview mirror for irate drivers—I had just stopped without apparent reason in the middle of the street—I turned my whole body to look over my shoulder. Not a soul was behind us.

No irate drivers...but in my back seat was one very agitated German shorthaired pointer. I wasn't backing up, because backing up was a very bad idea.

I knew what that vibrating tail and intense focus indicated, and I wanted no part of it.

"No. I am *not* turning down Bluebonnet. We're calling the police." I didn't usually call Chief Charleston when I was in a pinch, but desperate times...

"You mean the sheriff," she corrected me with a placid expression.

Helen knew I didn't want to call the sheriff, a.k.a.

Luke McCord, a.k.a. my something complicated, a.k.a. *not* my boyfriend...maybe. She may not have known the specifics, but she knew something was up.

"I didn't mean the sheriff. I meant Chief Charleston." And now someone *was* behind me. Since this was small-town Central Texas, that somebody didn't honk the horn of their massive truck. They waited patiently for me to sort myself out...while I was stopped in the middle of the street. Bless White Sage residents and their very un-Austin-like driving behavior.

I gestured for the driver of the truck to pass, and a very polite farmer lifted his hand in a pleasant wave as he drove by.

When I didn't immediately back up, Helen said, "We're not calling Luke or Bubba Charleston. Not until you turn down Bluebonnet and see what has Fairmont in a tizzy."

A woof and the scrabbling sound of claws on the interior of my door followed.

If I didn't know better, I'd swear that dog spoke English.

I shouldn't turn down Bluebonnet Lane. I didn't want to, but I also didn't see a sound alternative. If I did call the chief, what would I say? "Fairmont was acting oddly. Can you please come and investigate? Because I don't want to find a dead body."

Another dead body.

There really wasn't a choice. I needed to follow my dog's nose and see if something untoward awaited us.

Something untoward. Now there was a nice euphemism for a corpse. I shrugged my shoulders in an attempt to release some of the tension that had gathered there.

Maybe there was a squirrel. Fairmont had a special love-hate relationship with squirrels. And if a particularly cheeky squirrel had taunted him, he could get agitated.

Probably not this agitated—Fairmont was such a gentleman, the very best of dogs—but I held out hope.

Or wallowed in denial.

Whichever.

And I wouldn't get emotional over how wonderful Fairmont was. How much he meant to me. What an important part of my life he'd become.

My eyes burned, and that was *not* how one approached a potential crisis. I inhaled a cleansing breath, tucked away my feelings for the dog who had become such an integral part of my life, and turned down Bluebonnet Lane.

As Fairmont vibrated with excitement in the back, I watched to see where his nose pointed, hoping he'd caught a distant whiff of trouble.

He hadn't. His nose pointed to the shared back parking lot of Catie's Cupcakery and Sally's Sandwich Shoppe.

Why did it have to be Sally and Catie's parking lot?

Then the barking started, and with the sharp, repetitive barks, the "something untoward" we'd driven toward crystalized as a full-blown crisis.

As calmly as I could, I parked. I ignored Fairmont's excited woofs until I'd safely engaged the emergency brake. Then I turned around in my seat and called him. Once I had hold of his collar, he quieted.

That was when Helen spoke, confirming what I already knew to be true.

"There's a body here somewhere. The question now is, do we wait in the car and call Luke? Or do we let Fairmont find it and then call Luke?"

Nowhere in that equation was the option of calling Chief Charleston.

And as frustrated as I was right now with Luke—or my relationship with Luke...or the dynamics of my relationship with Luke—I also wanted his big, comforting, capable presence here. Right now. Before either one of us left this car.

"Helen Granger, don't you dare open that door." I pulled my phone out of its hands-free cradle.

"So, we're calling Luke?"

I didn't answer, but I did call Luke.

He picked up on the first ring. "Thank goodness. I wanted to talk to you about last night. I didn't—"

"I think Fairmont just found a body." I bit my lip.

"Are you safe?" he asked. All the warm intimacy that had been in his voice disappeared, replaced by the cool, calm tones of Sage County's sheriff.

I hated that my heart went pitter-patter over the fact that the very first question he asked was whether I was safe. Silly, because that was probably just basic law enforcement training.

"I'm safe. Helen's with me. We're in my car, parked behind—"

Oh. Oh, no. A cold wave washed over me, and my vision narrowed. I was parked behind Sally's place. Sally, who was Annie's mom, my friend, but, most importantly, Luke's sister.

"Zella?" Luke's voice, firm and calm, came across the line. "Where are you?"

I tried to speak, but a frog stole my voice. I cleared my throat, thinking as I did, formulating words. The right words. "Luke, I'm sorry. I'm gonna call you right back. Helen and I are safe. I'll call you right back."

And I hung up on him as he protested.

I shared a glance with Helen, who—clever woman—understood immediately. We both got out of the car at the same time. I pointed to the entrance of the parking lot.

Not that many cars would be in the area at six in the morning, but I wanted to be sure that Fairmont and I were safe.

Once she placed herself in a position to redirect any cars headed into the lot and I made certain that my cell phone was in the back pocket of my jeans, I opened the rear hatch and attached Fairmont's leash. He didn't seem to mind that my hands shook.

A week ago, I'd started lifting him out of the back of the SUV after he'd tweaked his elbow. He was better now, but I was glad I'd kept the habit. Holding an armful of warm dog settled my nerves a little. I set him carefully on the ground, held his collar, and then let out the leash slowly as he pulled on it. My hope was that he'd remember I was still attached and not drag me willy-nilly across the pavement.

It seemed to work. Moving at a steady trot but no more, he made a beeline for the dumpster that Sally, Catie, and one other business shared. He circled it, then jumped up and put his paws on it. He lingered just long enough for me to see that there was trash and only trash inside, then continued past it and into the alley behind the parking lot.

I jogged behind him, not minding my footing as well as I should, because I couldn't take my eyes off him. I stumbled once, then again, but never fell to my knees.

I was terrified of what he'd discover. *Who* he'd discover.

And not in a general sense, though having happened upon more than one dead person certainly hadn't made me immune to the horror of it.

I'd never seen the body of someone I cared for outside of a funeral home. And I very much wanted this poor person, whoever they might be, to be a stranger.

Someone unknown.

Someone I didn't care for.

Not Luke's sister.

I gasped for breath. He would be devastated.

Fairmont and I followed the alley for a short distance—perhaps the length of one or two shops—then crossed it.

Fairmont slowed to examine some scrubby vegetation, then he darted for some overgrown shrubs.

And barked.

I'd swear my heart stopped with the sound, and when it started beating again, it fluttered like a frantic, trapped bird as Fairmont's barks continued to sound in the otherwise quiet morning air.

I had to look. I had to know who he'd found. And I had to keep Fairmont away, just in case... The word "murder" fluttered through my mind and then escaped, because I was reeling in Fairmont, hushing him, kneeling, looking—

"Oh, Catie, no. No."

With her wide, unseeing eyes on me and the metallic scent of blood in my nose, I could barely get my trembling fingers to call Luke.

"Where are you?"

"I found Catie Smithart. She's dead, Luke."

With more patience than I would have had in the situation, he repeated, "Where are you?"

"Uh..." I looked up, because I hadn't a clue. "A dentist's office. The one that's across the alley from Catie and Sally's parking lot. That's where I parked. Helen's still there."

I recognized the sound of his work SUV starting as he replied, "I'm on my way."

2

The scent of death teases me.

I press my nose to the crack in the window. I catch traces, a hint, more.

There is death near. Fresh death. New death. Blood.

My lady leashes me, readies me for the search. My body fills with the excitement of the hunt.

But I am careful. I would not hurt Zella.

I am focused.

I am searching.

I am hunting.

And I am victorious!

3

Luke kept me on the phone while he drove. Other than a brief moment when he'd called for backup on his radio, he talked to me. Updating me on where he was, telling me what he had for breakfast, guessing I hadn't eaten yet, and even giving me the weather forecast.

He knew I just needed to hear his voice.

The fact that Luke understood I needed his support and intuited how best to give it as I waited, ten feet from the body of a woman I knew and liked, let me put aside our issues. For now. Because...Catie.

Oh, Catie.

I didn't look directly at her as I spoke.

This day, this awful day, had just become so much more terrible.

Luke told me he was letting me go because

Deputy Zapata was arriving, and he needed to make another call.

After I pocketed my phone, I kneeled down and hugged Fairmont, remembering belatedly that he'd done his job and hadn't received an ounce of the praise he deserved.

"You're the best dog," I murmured as I hugged him. "The very best."

The vibrating excitement he'd displayed since I'd pulled him away from the body stilled with a final shudder. He leaned into me and let me lavish him with pets and words of love.

"You are so smart. The smartest dog ever."

I could feel his butt wiggle as I continued to heap on praise and rub his chest.

Catie was just on the edge of my vision. I couldn't turn my back on her. It felt wrong, disrespectful, and yet I couldn't look directly at her.

Everything about her had been wrong.

Catie had been like her cupcakes. Sweet, fun, and unique.

Her rose-gold hair, normally a pretty complement to her fair skin, no longer brought out the pink in her cheeks. There was no color in her face at all.

And while she hadn't been gorgeous, her warm personality, ready smile, and animated hand gestures made her pretty.

There was nothing pretty about her still, pale form or her unseeing eyes.

And the blood.

There was so much blood. Enough that Fairmont had picked up the scent through the cracked window of my car a few blocks away.

There could be no question. Catie Smithart, White Sage's outgoing, bubbly baker, had been murdered.

"Ms. Marek?" Deputy Dave Zapata jogged into view.

"Zella," I reminded him as I stood. "Hi, Dave."

He blushed. Because I called him by his first name? Because he knew about Luke and me? But then his tawny golden skin paled, and I didn't have to follow the direction of his gaze to discover the reason why.

"Catie? From Catie's Cupcakery?" His voice wavered.

Dave Zapata was a fan of Catie's cupcakes. Most of White Sage was.

Her new business had flourished practically from the moment she'd opened her doors. Most of her income had likely come from weekenders and tourists, but she'd had strong support in the local community as well.

I didn't reply to Dave, because clearly it was Catie. Also, I was struggling to keep it together. I was solid in a crisis, but the aftermath could be worse. After a crisis, when stress and need weren't pushing me, that part could be harder.

While I'd been worried about a panicked Luke driving across town, not knowing whether the body behind Sally's shop was his sister's, I'd been the capable woman a crisis required. I'd put on a brave face and pretended courage I wasn't sure I had, because I simply couldn't allow the possibility of his sister's death to enter Luke's head.

But now... Now I wanted to cry. Because I'd had a not-great night, followed by a pretty terrible morning, and that had been before I realized White Sage had lost its favorite baker. Before I'd been confronted with the nasty reality of the terrible things people in this world did to one another. Before I'd seen all the blood.

The soft fur of Fairmont's head brushed against my fingers. I rubbed his ears, hoping he was getting as much comfort as he was giving.

Dave cleared his throat. "Ms. Marek, uh, Zella, did you touch anything?"

I shook my head. "Fairmont got close and might have nudged her." I closed my eyes. *Poor Catie.* I opened them to find Dave standing between me and Catie, blocking my view. "There's, ah, no blood on him. I checked. But Dave? I haven't had a moment to call Helen. Someone needs to check on her and let her know what's happened."

"Luke's taken care of that. What time did you arrive?"

Thank goodness for Luke's good sense and training. I'd left Helen waiting for news, but I could hardly hang up on Luke when his voice had been the one thing to keep me grounded.

"I don't know, maybe around six thirty? But I called Luke just as soon as I pulled into the lot behind the Cupcakery and again when I found Catie."

Except I hadn't found Catie. Not truly. I'd found a body. Catie was gone.

Her infectious laugh, her delicious cupcakes with the playful flavor pairings, her welcoming smile —all gone.

And that was when the adrenaline crash hit me hard.

I cried. I didn't sob or hiccup. There wasn't an excess of snot. But my eyes burned like they were on fire, and tears slipped down my cheeks.

Fairmont's warm body leaned against my legs.

Dave's face pinched, and for a second, I thought he might join me, but then I realized what I was seeing was dismay. Dave didn't know how to handle a silently crying witness.

He pressed his lips together and flipped his notebook shut. "Luke will be here in another minute or two. Can you wait for him, or do you need to go back to the car with Helen?"

Dave Zapata had learned a lot in the short time I'd lived in White Sage. I wiped my tears away, because really, it just wasn't the time, and I smiled at him. He was trying, and I appreciated it.

"Is someone with Helen?" When Dave assured me another deputy was with her, I said, "I'll wait until Luke gets here."

Which was my second brave act of the day. As much as I wanted to see Luke, I equally wanted to avoid him after how we'd left things last night. But he'd need to ask me more questions, and I wanted to help.

It was on the tail of those muddled thoughts that Luke appeared.

His gaze swept the scene, taking it all in—my tear-streaked face, Fairmont leaning supportively against me, Catie's body just a few feet away—and then he pulled me against his chest.

Speaking over my head, he gave Dave instructions, but I wasn't paying attention to anything he said. I let myself be held. I melted against his warmth. I allowed his solid form to give me strength.

And I didn't even feel weak or over-emotional. I just felt like a woman having a bad day who was relying on her friend. Luke and I *were* friends, however complicated other aspects of our relationship might be.

He held me quietly for what had to be several minutes, and when he eventually spoke, it wasn't at all what I expected. He didn't ask about Catie...or last night. "You sent the emails?"

Sometimes, the man was downright psychic.

"Yes, early this morning." I glanced down at Fairmont, now sitting next to me.

I'd reached a difficult decision in the last few days, and this morning around five, when sleep had eluded me, I'd drafted a careful email and sent it to every search-and-rescue organization in the state. I'd inquired if any of their team members or anyone within their circle of acquaintance had lost a trained search dog in the last six months.

I hadn't included many details, not breed or age and certainly no pictures, but I'd explained that I suspected my adopted dog had SAR training and that I felt obligated to reach out to the search community in case someone's search dog had gone missing.

My heart had felt like it was breaking as I'd sent those emails.

There'd been too much heartache today. I inhaled deeply. I knew what Luke was doing. He was trying to get me thinking about something, anything, other than Catie. Giving me a moment to regroup before he started the questions.

How terrible was it that speaking about Fairmont's future—the topic most likely to raise my blood pressure only twenty minutes ago—was now a "safe" topic?

"It's been a tough day." But not more than I could handle. I could do this. "Helen and I were headed to Catie's this morning. We were hoping she'd let us sneak in and grab an early batch of cupcakes."

"I'm sure she would have."

I stepped back from Luke and his solid, warm comfort. He'd taken Fairmont's leash from me at some point, and he handed it back now.

He reached down and petted Fairmont, and when another patrol car pulled into the dentist's parking lot, he said, "Dave's going to escort you back to Helen and your car. I'll come by later and take your statement, but if there's anything you want to tell me before you go..."

So no questioning. That was surprising.

"The dumpster," I replied automatically. "Fairmont was interested in the dumpster."

And because Fairmont was special, because he wasn't your average trash hound, ready to snatch any smelly item from the garbage, Luke said, "We'll check it out."

Then he gave Fairmont a final pet and waved over Dave.

Five minutes later, I was in the passenger seat of my own car being driven away from the scene of a crime by Helen.

She'd looked shell-shocked to me, a fact I'd pointed out when she offered to drive. She'd given me a pointed look and said, "You should have a look at yourself, sweet cheeks."

A comment that had the intended result. I'd smiled, however weakly, and handed over my keys.

"Wait," I said as she turned down Main. "We can't go home."

The weight of Fairmont's chin resting on my shoulder reminded me that I owed a certain dog a special treat for his hard work.

Helen slowed and waited for me to elaborate.

I rubbed Fairmont's ears. "Sonic? Do you think they'd be open?"

"Not yet, but The Drip will be. I'd planned on pitching it anyway. I don't think heading home by yourself right now is a great idea. Breakfast, on the other hand, is always an excellent plan."

I'd been thinking more along the lines of a plain and dry burger for Fairmont when I'd mentioned Sonic. But The Drip had egg white and turkey bacon sandwiches. That would do in a pinch, since they made them on site and could leave off the extras.

And Fairmont was welcome on their patio. "Sure. Let's hit The Drip."

When we arrived, the parking lot was almost empty. A few regulars ate an early breakfast, but most early customers at The Drip didn't linger. They grabbed their coffee and hustled out the door, eager to get on the road and get their day started. There were a handful of telecommuters cropping up in White Sage and North Sage Grove, because internet service was good in both towns, but they were more likely to hit The Drip at nine or ten o'clock.

One car in the lot stood out. A Ford Bronco of indeterminate age with flat blue paint.

Ever since Vanessa had become less and less reliant on her cane, she'd started to drive her deceased husband's SUV. It happened to also be her only vehicle now that she'd sold her little sedan. Georgie, her sister-in-law, best friend, and coauthor, had previously assumed the bulk of the driving when they'd run about town together.

I wasn't sure if Vanessa was trying to repay her dear friend's efforts by taking on more of the driving or if she simply enjoyed puttering around town in the car she'd rediscovered.

Helen parked the Grand Cherokee three spaces over from the blue beast. Vanessa might be able to get in and out of the truck, but she wasn't the best at parking. Or reversing. Or navigating tight spaces in general.

"Why is Vanessa's Bronco here?"

"I'd have thought that was obvious: Vanessa is here." Helen smiled softly. "And Georgie. I called them a few minutes before you got back to the car. Like I said, I didn't want you home alone right now, and everyone thought breakfast at The Drip was a great idea."

The Sleuthing Granny Gang—comprised of Helen, Vanessa, and Georgie—was always trying to feed me.

"I do manage to eat without being prodded." I idly rubbed Fairmont's ears. Once the SUV had stopped, he'd stood up and put his chin on my shoulder again.

"On a normal day," Helen replied.

Today certainly wasn't that.

I looked at Helen closely, searching for signs of shock or overt distress. She'd liked Catie. I knew because she'd told me as much more than once. She seemed calm. Purposeful, but that was her normal state of being.

Helen was a fan of Catie's, and Georgie liked just about everyone. Even Vanessa, with her finicky culinary tastes, had enjoyed Catie's cupcakes and had a kind word for her. It helped that Catie hadn't ventured into the realm of pie baking. No one's pies were as good as Vanessa's.

But the point was that each of the three women had a connection to Catie and a fondness for her.

Three women, who were very good friends, had set up a breakfast meeting to support me and each other in our mutual grief.

That was one interpretation.

A more likely scenario, still rooted in their affection for Catie, was that they'd decided to tackle the case.

As Helen gathered her purse, I hovered with the door open. I almost told her this meeting was a bad idea, but I didn't.

Not because I thought hunting Catie's killer was a *good* idea.

It wasn't. It was, in fact, a *terrible* idea.

No, the reason I kept my silence as I exited the car and retrieved Fairmont was because I knew my withdrawal from the SGG's shenanigans wouldn't stop them. They'd simply meet without me. Dig around in the underbelly of White Sage without me.

Three senior ladies, running around White Sage, poking their noses into the business of a violent killer. If that wasn't enough to make my chest tighten with anxiety, then the vision that popped into my head of Catie's body, of all the blood, certainly was.

Whoever had done *that* couldn't be allowed anywhere near my sweet elderly friends.

I rested my hand against the Grand Cherokee. I needed just a moment to catch my breath.

No, I wouldn't refuse to participate in this investigation, because those three lovely ladies needed me. I was the sane counterbalance to their wildly inappropriate desire for adventure.

Set on my course of action, I pushed myself away from my car and followed Helen into The Drip.

As I watched her stride purposefully to the back patio, I couldn't help but wonder if I'd ever be as bold as her.

Helen blamed my ongoing objections to the SGG's "investigations" on PHCS, Post-Helen-Concussion Syndrome, and I'd have to agree. Having my senior friend conked on the head, suffer a concussion, and spend several days in the hospital made me wary of further injury. And not just to Helen. Vanessa and Georgie weren't spring chickens, either. Something as simple as a shove could have serious medical consequences.

But even after her hospital stay, Helen was as determined as ever to right wrongs, solve crimes, and be fully immersed in every aspect of White Sage's unsavory element.

She'd been the impetus behind the SGG, though all responsibility for the name was my own.

The naming of the group turned out to be ironic, since Helen had been the only grandmother at the time. Not for long.

In the last week, I'd learned that my daughter was expecting her first child. *I* was going to be a grandmother.

I paused at the gate to the outdoor seating area. *I'm going to be a grandmother.*

In his excitement at seeing his friends, Fairmont didn't realize I'd stopped and hit the end of the leash. He glanced back with a reproachful look in his brown eyes, and I continued forward.

I hadn't told the ladies of Greta's pregnancy, and I didn't plan to this morning. It wasn't the time. But I would. Soon.

A thought occurred. One accompanied by a touch of guilt. Maybe an investigation wouldn't be such a terrible thing right now?

There was turmoil and uncertainty surrounding so many of the important relationships in my life: Fairmont, Luke, and both my children, Greta and Mark.

If the SGG was going to be involved, maybe I could take the lead for a change. Keep my vulnerable friends out of harm's way...and focus my attention on something bigger, more important, than my own worries.

Georgie waved a hanky when she spotted us.

"You made our murder meeting."

It looked like Georgie had been crying, if the lacy scrap of cloth and her red eyes were any indication. And when she said "murder," her eyes welled up.

Vanessa scanned the patio with a grim look, as if other patrons would be lurking there on a chilly mid-October day. Squeezing Georgie's arm in support, she said, "We shouldn't announce to the world why we're meeting. In case word isn't out yet about..." She trailed off, avoiding the word "murder." "Anyway, we're glad you could come, Zella."

I greeted them as I attached Fairmont's leash to the sturdy picnic table leg. I placed the small but nicely padded foam bathmat I'd toted from the car on the ground, and Fairmont immediately curled up in a ball on top of it.

"It is, isn't it?" Georgie blinked red-rimmed eyes at me. "A murder?" she whispered.

Helen wouldn't have known when she called them. I'd told her in the car. But already the word was out. Such was the way of White Sage gossip. Erratic, yes, and not always accurate, but frighteningly fast.

Helen nodded, and Georgie's eyes welled up again.

I couldn't watch her cry. I hated that about myself, but I was a sympathy crier. If someone else got teary, then I got teary. You'd think raising two toddlers with all their tantrums would have dried my sympathy tears forever, and yet, no.

"Keep an eye on Fairmont while I run inside and order?" I asked.

All three ladies enthusiastically agreed. I was still half-convinced I only belonged to their sleuthing group because of Fairmont.

I took their orders—Georgie and Vanessa had only just arrived and hadn't ordered yet—then went inside to confront my nemesis.

Liam gave me a sheepish look, as he did each time I came into The Drip. I'd probably tortured him enough by keeping silent, and it was just a little bit funny that in this skinny, goateed nineteen-year-old, I'd discovered one of the cogs of the White Sage gossip machine.

After he took my order and I'd paid, I said, "I don't bite." I paused, then added, "Or hold grudges...much."

His eyebrows flew up, and then he blushed. I didn't miss nineteen, with all its awkwardness and uncertainty.

He blinked, then smiled, but the pink on his cheeks didn't fade. "I'm really sorry I ratted you out to my dad that one time. I didn't mean to cause you any problems."

And this was the source of whatever perceived enmity he believed existed between us. He'd tattled to his dad, who happened to be a friend of Luke's, that Helen and I were plotting mayhem in The Drip. Since this had occurred after Luke had encouraged both Helen and me not to involve ourselves, and his dad happened to see Luke that day, I'd gotten a mild scolding from Luke in his capacity as sheriff.

I really didn't hold a grudge. You'd think poor Liam would realize that, since I tipped him every time I came in.

But then, guilt could color a person's perspective.

I grinned at him. He was a good kid. "Are you going to call your dad today?"

"No," he replied, dead earnest. "Your business is your business." His lips twitched. "And I really appreciate the tips. I'm taking business courses at the community college, and tips fund my textbooks."

Thank you, Liam, for sharing the key to your continued silence. I made a note to keep the tips rolling.

It wasn't until he'd finished two drinks—my latte with hemp milk and Helen's herbal tea—and delivered them to me at the counter he asked, "What's brought you ladies in today? We've been mystery-free for a few weeks now."

I'd assumed he knew. But if law enforcement hadn't been in for coffee... Well, I didn't actually know how all of White Sage's gossip cogs worked together to create its stream of information.

And now I had to tell a kid barely out of high school that someone had been murdered. Actually, no. Not the murdered part. But it seemed best to tell him she'd died. Who knew how he'd hear the information?

"Liam, I'm not sure if you knew Catie Smithart personally, but—" His face lost all color. I thought he might be close to passing out, so I leaned across the counter and gripped his arm tightly.

"What happened to Catie?"

Still gripping his arm, I said the words that my expression and tone must have already given away, given his reaction. "She's dead, Liam."

4

I waited until Liam's color improved before I returned to the patio. He refused any help and insisted that he'd deliver our remaining drinks and food when they were ready, so there wasn't much more I could do.

"What do we know about Liam?" I asked as I sat down. I gave Fairmont a quick scratch under the chin, and he settled back on his mat. "He's coming with your French press and mugs, Georgie and Vanessa, and I don't think it will take him long. He had a very strong reaction to the news of Catie's death."

Helen hopped right in. "His father, Noah, is friends with Luke. That much you know. He lives at home, goes to community college, though I'm not sure what he's studying."

"Business," I replied.

"Ah." Vanessa nodded. "His aunt owns The Drip. I wonder if he might be hoping to take over management, since she's dating that man up in Dallas now."

That made sense. I hadn't known his aunt owned The Drip. "Okay, but what about Catie? How does he know Catie?"

No one replied. The telltale creak of the patio entrance to The Drip announced Liam's imminent arrival.

He dropped off the large French press, two mugs, a small pitcher of cream, and a sugar bowl. I knew from experience it contained cubed sugar. Probably some kind of health code violation, but I loved it nonetheless.

"Thank you, Liam." Helen's sharp eyes locked in on him.

He didn't make eye contact with her—or any of us except Fairmont—merely clutched the serving tray to his chest, forced a smile, then disappeared.

As soon as the door thunked shut, Helen said, "Well, he can't be dating her, because he's dating Annie."

"Wait, what?" There was so much confusing in that sentence that I didn't know where to start. No, I did know. "I thought Annie was dating Vince, the pizza delivery boy."

Vanessa made a dismissive noise. "That was

weeks ago. Or ten days." She must have spotted my incredulity, because she said, "Pay attention, Zella. When the pizza boy looks like someone's confiscated all his secret naked lady magazines, you should ask him what's wrong."

It took me a second to realize that a young man who's had his girlie mags nabbed might look perhaps...sad?

"Zella doesn't order pizza, Nessa." Georgie rolled her eyes, as if everyone should know that.

She wasn't wrong. I usually stayed away from it. Unlike Helen, I couldn't eat three thousand calories a day without gaining weight.

But for the stress of the murder investigations I'd been privy to, I probably would have put on a good ten pounds since I moved here. Helen had been spot on with her earlier accusation that I forgot to eat when I was under pressure or very busy. Forgot...or reverted to old, very bad habits.

Georgie wagged a finger at her friend. "You shouldn't be ordering pizza. It's not good for your cholesterol. All that cheese."

Vanessa shrugged. "I order thin crust, half cheese, with veggie toppings. But that's not the point. My point was that Liam doesn't have a romantic attachment to Catie."

I wasn't even going to address the fact that Catie was easily in her late twenties, maybe even early thirties, and Liam was nineteen. Romance wasn't the first conclusion I'd have drawn.

"I was glad when I heard about Liam and Annie. He's such a good boy." This from Helen, who'd given him the evil eye for several visits after he'd ratted us out to Luke via his dad.

But I couldn't argue. The little I knew of Liam pointed to him being a good kid. And I could spot a troublemaker at ten paces.

Greta spent the end of high school and beginning of college dating the naughty-verging-on-future-criminal types, so I had a few years of training under my belt. Actually, I should thank my stars that she'd settled into a loving relationship before getting herself knocked up.

Oh my, that was an uncharitable thought. Perhaps to do with my conflicted feelings related to becoming a grandmother. I was excited: my child would experience the joy of raising her own child. But also worried: there were so many health risks. And then there was the idea that I was going to be a *grandmother*. Something I'd always equated with being *old*. And yet, I'd have a little person to love and adore and spoil. So many feelings...

I turned my attention back to the matter at hand. Liam. And Annie.

"So Liam and Annie are dating now?" I asked.

A cleared throat, not from the ladies at the table,

informed me of my mistake. I'd failed to register the sound of the patio door opening.

As Liam delivered our orders, he said, "Annie and I went out a few weeks ago and started dating exclusively just recently."

It was a very grown-up answer ruined by the hot pink that covered his cheekbones and traveled all the way to the tips of his ears.

I rested my hand lightly on his arm. "I'm glad to hear that. Annie deserves a nice young man."

Which just ratcheted up his embarrassment and his bright coloring, but he took my comment as the compliment it was and replied accordingly. "Thank you. I really like her."

They were both so young. But then... Were they really? I'd been married when I was only a little older than Liam.

Much as I hated where my marriage had ended, it had begun beautifully: bright and hopeful, with two young people in love. And that marriage had given me Greta and Mark, my two wonderful—though occasionally selfish—children.

"I'll be back as soon as I finish Fairmont's order. I have to make it from scratch, so it'll be a few minutes."

Our other orders had come straight off the menu, so Liam had likely made them this morning and only had to reheat them. Which was when I realized the connection between Liam, or The Drip, and Catie.

"Liam," I said, very softly. "Did Catie bake the bread for The Drip before she opened up her cupcake shop?"

"Yeah. She used to deliver every morning before we opened, back when she was still using Sally's kitchen." He swallowed. "She was really cool."

He hesitated, and rather than ask him a question or fill the silence, I waited. My children had taught me that sullen silences, tortured silences, angry silences all served a function, and rushing their conclusion wasn't to my advantage.

The Sleuthing Granny Gang agreed, because I could almost feel the questions they were swallowing.

After several heartbeats, our patience bore fruit. "She's the one who convinced me to start taking classes at the community college," Liam said. "She even helped me fill out the admissions paperwork and make a budget so I could decide if I should try to get a loan or pay my way by staying on here at The Drip full-time."

I wouldn't have guessed she'd do such a thing, but I wasn't surprised.

"I'm really sorry that you lost your friend." I could feel the burn of sympathetic tears in my eyes. But I wouldn't cry. If I did, then Liam might, and he wouldn't appreciate that at all, especially at work.

"Thanks." Then he hurried away before we could ask him another unwelcome question about the woman who'd touched his life and was now gone.

"Thank goodness for Annie. She'll see him right." Helen had her phone out and was texting. "There. I've sent her a note to check in with Liam, but not to make a fuss."

As soon as she set her phone down, it rang. Guaranteed it was a confused Annie looking for clarification. Interpreting Helen's texts was like translating toddler speech. Practice was key, and I was guessing Annie had little.

Helen silenced her ringer then frowned at me. "Don't look that way. We're conducting a meeting. We have several agenda items."

I had an inkling that I might be one of the agenda items. I reached my hand out, palm up, and waited for her to relinquish her phone.

When I swiped the screen, I found it unlocked. "We talked about this. You need to password-protect your phone, Helen." Both Vanessa and Georgie agreed and then proceeded to outline nightmare stolen phone scenarios as they poured their coffee and I translated Helen's garbled message.

I typed out a much clearer one for Annie, signing

my name to it. Seconds after I sent it, I got a smiley face and thanks.

Neither Helen nor I had mentioned Catie's death, because text was hardly the way to do it. But at least now Annie knew to check in with Liam. That boy needed a hug, and as Helen had said, Annie would see him right.

By the time I returned the phone, the issue of phone security had been exhausted and all three women were giving me the Look. Worse, they were letting their food go cold, which implied a level of commitment that might be problematic.

"I thought this was a murder meeting." My stomach flipped when I said "murder," but I made myself pick up my hemp latte and sip it. Finding it cool enough to drink quickly, I busied myself putting a dent in my morning caffeine deficit.

Vanessa squinted at me. She might need readers, but at this distance her vision was more than adequate. She was making a point. "We're women. We multitask well."

This had to be about Fairmont. Helen knew I'd sent the emails. I told her this morning.

I couldn't just ring a friend before her morning coffee, beg her presence for a cupcake raid, and not explain why my emotional state required the immediate consumption of sugar, butter, and flour. It wasn't done.

Georgie gave me a stern look. It wasn't a natural state of being for Georgie, and all the more effective as a result. "We need to discuss your children."

Not what I'd been expecting. I'd just turned to my egg white and spinach omelet when Georgie spoke. My appetite for sweets had faded with the morning's events—and now the omelet wasn't looking so great.

Also, did the walls have ears? How did anyone outside of Luke know about my children's recent shenanigans? I suspected a social media leak. Not Greta, probably not Mark, but maybe my ex or his new wife?

I relayed none of this, because I didn't want to discuss it.

All I said was: "Ah."

Georgie frowned. "You're a grown woman."

"I am."

Her eyebrows flew up in surprise. Was she expecting me to disagree?

Vanessa, still squinting, said, "Your life is yours to live as you see fit."

I was hardly going to argue with her, so I nodded as I continued to down my latte.

But it was Helen, ever brash and practical, who got down to business. "All right, then, if that's true, explain to us what's going on with you and Luke. You're fighting over your kids."

I could tell from her expression that the last part had been a guess. She didn't *know* we were fighting, merely intuited it.

"Luke and I aren't fighting." We *were* fighting, but I didn't want to tell my friends that. They were loyal. They'd take my side, and I didn't think sides needed to be taken. Not about this.

I was frustrated with him. He was trying to be patient—the man's patience was practically legendary—but I was starting to see the edges of that epic patience fray. "And how are we talking about this right now? What about Catie?"

Helen's lips pinched, and I realized how low that was. We'd all liked Catie. A lot. She would be missed, and her absence was made so, so much worse by the fact that someone had taken her from us.

If my ladies needed a few minutes' distraction before they tackled their latest, very personal, project, then I'd give it to them.

"I'm not sure exactly what you think you know, but here's the long and short of it," I said. "My ex's new wife and my daughter are both expecting."

I could tell from their expressions that this, at least, was news.

"Oh, how exciting." Georgie beamed. "You'll be a grandmother. You must be so excited."

"Awkward," Vanessa murmured. When she

spotted Georgie scowling at her, she added, "Ah, congratulations."

"No, Vanessa, you're right. Awkward is the understatement of the decade." I smiled grimly. "Both of my children seem to be trying very, very hard to deal with their father's changed circumstance, and..." This was the difficult part. This was the part that Luke didn't understand. Wouldn't try to understand. "And that seems to have exhausted their emotional reserve."

"That's a bunch of hooey," Helen said with great conviction. As the only other woman at the table with children, that stung.

"Greta is hormonal like you wouldn't believe. Mark is finally in a stable relationship, which means that he's feeling pressure to propose, and I know that's created a lot of stress for him." I paused, because I wasn't sure how to say this in a way that didn't paint my children as the selfish little twits they were temporarily acting like. "They're having a difficult time with the idea of me dating."

"But Luke is hot," Georgie said with big puppy-dog eyes. "And really nice. And he makes you happy."

Georgie, sweet, sweet Georgie, would of course hit the nail right on the head. My children should only care that Luke made me happy, and yet...

Vanessa took that theme and ran with it. "Your

husband cheated on *you*. You had the courage to end a lengthy, unhappy marriage, which was no easy change, but the right thing for your well-being. And then you moved to a place where you could be happier and healthier." She resumed the squint that had fallen away. "We don't think your previous life was very healthy."

"Or that you had very nice friends," Georgie added softly.

Since I'd only occasionally mentioned my friend group there, I had to wonder how she knew that. She was right, but I wasn't sure *how* she was right. The peer pressure had been terrible, and my friendships quite shallow. That lifestyle wasn't one I'd ever want to return to.

"Your children should see how much better everything is for you here," Helen said, summing up the group's sentiments in one sweeping statement.

"But they should especially appreciate Luke," Georgie said. With that twinkle in her eye, I now had a pretty good idea which of the two ladies was responsible for the romantic content of their cowritten mysteries.

Luke hadn't touched on my previous lifestyle last night—which had at times crossed a line into the unhealthy—or my former friends. But he had flat-out told me that my children were being selfish.

And they were.

They refused to meet Luke. They criticized my relationship with him. They told me I shouldn't be dating a younger man. Or someone in law enforcement. Or someone in the tiny hick town I'd moved to.

My children were being little shits.

But they were my children, and I loved them. Even when they weren't their best selves.

And that was what I told the three lovely ladies sitting at the table with concern etched on their faces.

"Okay," Helen said, then tucked into her breakfast sandwich.

I pushed my cold omelet away. "Okay?"

"Uh-huh," she murmured around a bit of sandwich. Once she'd swallowed, she said, "But—"

I raised my eyebrows.

"I assume Luke's upset about this?" she said

I nodded. "He wants to meet my kids, and they basically told me where I can go when I mentioned it. I'm sure his feelings are hurt."

Vanessa snorted.

Georgie, who'd been widowed more years than she'd been married and, so far as I knew, hadn't dated in decades, patted my hand. "No, honey. That's not it at all. Luke's angry that you won't stand up for yourself."

Helen nodded. "And that you're letting your children treat you poorly."

"You know the saying about the goose and the gander?" Vanessa asked. "Your children are holding you to a terrible double standard. I assume they haven't fussed about your ex's new wife or the baby?"

Making eye contact wasn't going to happen. I couldn't look Vanessa—or any of them—in the eye and hide my anger. "They've come to terms with my husband's new wife and are thrilled about the addition to the family."

They weren't actually thrilled, but they did seem genuinely happy. And yet I wasn't allowed to even date. Thanks for that, kiddos.

Helen growled. An honest-to-goodness rumble that started in her chest and then left her pinched lips. "And that man cheated on you."

With his current wife, among others, but that bit of knowledge wouldn't hurry this conversation along.

My ex had been a terrible husband in the end. Actually, more like halfway through our marriage, if I was truthful. But he'd always been a pretty decent dad. Maybe that was why I was allowing my children to be selfish twits. Because I didn't want to stir the pot. I didn't want to upset the precarious balance that now existed between my ex, my children, his new wife, and their future half sibling.

But where did that leave me?

I inhaled. I knew exactly where it left me. With the murder of a dear woman and three sleuthing grannies who wouldn't let it rest.

After Catie's killer was caught, then I'd turn an eye to dealing with my children. Luke deserved the chance to meet them, if that was what he wanted.

And I deserved more than they were currently giving me. I deserved an ounce of the same consideration they'd been giving their philandering father and his twenty-something arm-candy wife. More than that, I deserved to find my own happiness, and that should bring them some comfort.

Hmm.

I might be a little bitter.

Best not to broach that topic with the kids until I had a handle on the pile of negative emotions surrounding it.

As those tumultuous thoughts rattled around in my head, Liam returned with Fairmont's sandwich.

"Sorry for the delay. Sheriff McCord, Deputy Zapata, and Deputy Sayers came in for coffee and a bite. I didn't think you'd mind them jumping in line, what with, ah..."

"Of course not," Helen told him, but she was looking at me.

Liam scarpered. Afraid of more questions or just

busy, either way, he escaped as quickly as he politely could.

And not thirty seconds later, before we'd even uttered a word about Luke's case, the man himself entered the patio looking decidedly grim.

"Ladies. What brings the four of you to The Drip this morning?"

Helen, being much more experienced in evading the scrutiny of the law, said, "You, Luke McCord. Well, you and Zella."

Before she had a chance to explain that we'd been dissecting my dysfunctional relationship with my children and the negative impact that was having on my romantic relationship with *him*, there was a screeching scrape of wood on concrete.

Fairmont, in his enthusiasm to greet one of his favorite people, had heaved the very heavy picnic table along the concrete pad that made up the floor of the patio.

My second favorite person!

Luke gives great pets.

And really good scratches.

And excellent neck rubs.

Luke isn't bothered by blood, and he thinks dead people are interesting. I bet he likes to hunt as much as I do.

If I had Zella, my favorite lady in the whole world, and *Luke, my life would be perfect.*

But even more important, I think Zella needs Luke. She's so much happier when Luke is home with us.

"Hey, buddy. I'm super excited to see you, too." Luke knelt and petted Fairmont, while simultaneously shoving him on the chest so he'd back up and create slack in his leash.

I quickly detached his leash from the leg of the picnic table.

"You'd think he hadn't seen you in weeks," Helen murmured.

Luke shot her a warning look. "He's a dog, Helen. He has no sense of time. Unlike you." He glanced at his watch. "How are you here, when just over an hour ago you were supposed to be taking Zella home?"

Which raised the question: how did Luke finish at the scene so quickly?

But I was too annoyed by his implication to ask

about the scene. Especially after the ladies had scolded me this morning for not standing up for myself. "Is Helen my keeper?" I said. "Or are you? I'm a grown woman. I can take care of myself." Even if I did forget to eat when I experienced high levels of stress.

Luke squeezed his eyes shut with a pained expression. I wasn't the only one who'd had a terrible morning. When he opened his eyes again, he just looked tired.

I stood up, handed Fairmont's leash to Helen, then tugged on Luke's arm. When he didn't budge, I said, "You were leaving, right?" He didn't argue, so I said, "I'm walking you to your car."

He took his time saying goodbye to Fairmont. There was something soothing about the velvety softness of my dog's ears, the happy light in his eyes when he was petted, and the enthusiastic wag of his stubby tail.

When he'd gotten his Fairmont fix, Luke stood. "Enjoy your breakfast, ladies." Then he left with me. It was completely out of character.

I wrapped my hand in his. "No warning to stay away from your investigation?"

"Would it do any good?" If he'd looked tired before, now he sounded defeated.

I stopped and really looked at him. My guy, who

was solid as a rock, always there for me with a phone call, a visit, a surprise meal, didn't look like himself.

This time it was me who hugged him. And he didn't hold me close to his chest or envelop me in his warmth like he normally did. He squeezed me tight, like he wanted to bury himself in my feel, my smell, my touch.

His arms loosened, and he kissed my temple. "Thank you."

I leaned back and looked at his face. "Do you want to tell me what's going on?"

"You mean besides the regular stuff? My girl-friend's children hate me even though they've never met me. They refuse to meet me, because they don't approve. Also, she's upset about possibly losing her dog."

"My kids are being selfish twits." Fairmont I wasn't ready to discuss.

His eyebrows flew up in surprise. I'd admitted as much to myself, but not to Luke.

Last night, when he'd brought up the idea of meeting my children, I'd fessed up that they didn't want to meet him. And then I'd defended the stinkers.

They really were going through a lot on the parental front right now. Their initial reaction to my ex's news of a new child hadn't been positive, especially on the heels of his marriage to a woman close in age to Greta.

They'd accepted Francie, the ex's new wife, without too much lingering fuss, and when I'd reminded them that her child would be their brother or sister, they'd toned down the whining about their dad's new addition.

Most of the bending I'd asked them to do was on their father's behalf, and not my own. And when I had asked for a little understanding in regard to my own life, they hadn't been nearly so readily swayed to the cause.

"I'll deal with my kids," I said. Luke's eyebrows climbed higher, so I answered his unasked question. "Soon."

He twined our fingers and then tipped his head toward his car.

I followed, but he wasn't getting away without answering my question. "Now, what's really wrong?"

Because as annoyed as he might be by the admittedly ridiculous reactions of my children to recent developments in my personal life, that wasn't at the heart of his distress.

We walked the remaining distance to his county-issued SUV in silence. When we arrived, he looked down at the keys in his hand. "I liked her. A lot." He smiled faintly. "She sent cupcakes to the office every other Friday. Bubba's office got them on our off weeks."

It wasn't the murder, so much as the murder victim.

I held back a sigh. "Everyone liked Catie."

He turned to me. "Yeah. That shouldn't matter. That everyone liked her, that she was popular, that she was young, that she was talented."

"She baked the best cupcakes I've ever eaten."

"It shouldn't matter, because she's a victim and deserves the same justice that every other victim does."

"But it makes it worse."

He shook his head, like he was going to disagree, but said, "It does."

Was he mad at himself because he cared more about Catie's case, because she was such a lovely person? I didn't think so. There was something I was missing.

Catie had been special. She hadn't lived in White Sage for long, and the town had embraced her. Even more so than they'd embraced Fairmont and me.

Which made me wonder... "Where was Catie from originally?"

All expression leached from Luke's face. If ever there was a cop face, this was it. He didn't reply. Maybe he couldn't. It was a murder investigation.

But how was Catie's hometown or previous residence confidential information? The White Sage gossip mill had to have ground up her past and spit it out to everyone in a twenty-mile radius. Except me, obviously, but that was no great surprise.

I hadn't quite plugged myself into all of the various information outlets. Helen usually only shared when I asked, and Georgie and Vanessa limited their gossip sessions to our murder meetings.

My mystery-writing friends were too busy crafting their next bestseller most days to share the gossip they gathered. And a good thing, too, because I was anxiously awaiting book ten in their most popular series. I could certainly do with the distraction from real-life woes.

"Never mind. I'll ask Helen."

Usually, a reminder that any information he was withholding was readily accessible to the entirety of White Sage was sufficient for Luke to share what he knew.

Not this time.

He kissed me on the cheek and told me to be safe. He didn't issue a warning to stay out of the investigation, because he knew that wasn't a reasonable request. Not with the SGG determined to participate.

Georgie and Vanessa, led by Helen, were an unstoppable force. They were the Sleuthing Granny

Gang, as they'd dubbed themselves after I made the mistake of revealing that was how I thought of our small circle.

They solved crime, and I usually tagged along hoping no one would be injured or worse. I was definitely the mom of the group. And like any mom, it was time to get a handle on the kids' shenanigans.

I waved as Luke drove away. The other deputies must have left when he'd joined all of us on the patio, because their cruisers were nowhere to be seen.

As I walked back to the patio, it occurred to me that Luke probably hadn't had time to inform Catie's next of kin of her passing. He still had that terrible task to complete, which made me regret not giving him another hug before he'd gotten in his SUV.

"What has you looking so grim?" Helen asked as I sat down.

Georgie tilted her head. "Murder?"

Helen's gaze sharpened as she examined me. "We're all upset about that. Catie was... Catie was special. But it's something else."

"Do any of you happen to know where Catie is from?" I reached down and ran my hand from Fairmont's head to the tip of his velvet-soft ear. He didn't open his eyes or move from his curled position on his mat, but his nub of a tail wagged slowly.

I continued to run my hand from his head to the

tip of his ear several times before I realized none of the ladies had replied. I looked up to find three pairs of eyes glued on me. "Wait, none of you know where Catie moved here from?" Silence. "Or where she grew up?" Not a peep. "Or what she did before she baked bread for Sally?"

"Sally!" Helen's eyes lit up. "We need to talk to Sally. What do we think, ladies? Is it time for lunch yet?"

I eyed my cold egg white omelet. "I'm in."

My breakfast only had a pinch of salt, and I hadn't had the chance to add pepper. I poked around to investigate the veggies and found them all dog-safe.

Fairmont's nose twitched as I lowered the plate in front of him, then his eyes popped open. Before I could blink, half the omelet was gone, and then he stood up to finish the rest.

"We can't go, Georgie." Vanessa folded her napkin and tucked it under her empty plate. "And we've both just eaten."

"But I want to go." Georgie sounded wistful, not as if she was objecting. She pulled a face and told Helen and me, "We're on a tight deadline for our book. And since we've already taken the morning..."

I snapped my fingers. "Facebook. Instagram, Twitter, all of those. You both know your way around social media, right?"

"I'm Facebook," Georgie replied. "Nessa is Instagram. She's much better with pictures than I am."

"We don't do Twitter," Vanessa added. "But I see where you're going. We'll poke around in between our writing sprints."

"Wait." Helen eyed them curiously. "You write *together*?"

Georgie looked confused. "We're coauthors."

"I understand that, but you physically write together? In the same room, at the same time?" Helen sounded about as confused as I was.

Vanessa sighed. "I dictate. Georgie translates as she types it up. Her grammar and typing are much better."

"But you're very good with details," Georgie said.

"And you're very good with the people," Vanessa replied.

Georgie considered this, then said, "No, I think we're both good with the people."

They were adorable. Between the two of them—Fairmont's reassuring chin resting on my knee, and Luke's hug—I was finally feeling more tethered. Earlier, I'd felt disconnected. Like I was here, but not entirely.

Even so, under my improved state of mind, the lingering sadness of a life lost remained.

I hadn't known Sylvester or Alice, previous victims of violence in White Sage. And not only had

I not known Pablo, but he'd seemed like the worst sort of person, a user and perhaps even a sociopath. Each of them had been a victim, but they'd been strangers to me. And while death of any sort was to be mourned, there was no comparison between the death of those strangers and the death of someone like Catie.

Helen patted my arm. "We'll figure this out. We'll find out who did this and why."

"And we'll find her people." Vanessa might not have children of her own, but she had the light of a determined mama bear in her eyes.

"And maybe we'll shoot him while we're at it." These last words were from a teary-eyed Georgie. Sweet, cheerful, optimistic Georgie...who also happened to have a concealed carry license.

I'd have a chat with Vanessa about relocating Georgie's firearm for the duration of this particular Sleuthing Granny Gang case.

7

Sally wasn't available.

Or rather, she had the highest level of security to screen access to her.

"But we just want a quick word," Helen said, smiling not-at-all-innocently at Annie.

Annie lifted her pen and order pad and repeated what she'd already said twice: "My mom's not available. Can I take your order?"

Helen narrowed her eyes. "Luke's gotten to you, hasn't he?"

Her implication being that Annie was knuckling under pressure applied by her uncle, as if Luke's primary concern in life was to prevent the SGG from interviewing witnesses. Sometimes, in her zeal, Helen missed the bigger picture.

Annie was a sweet kid. She adored her Uncle

Luke. I doubted she felt at all cowed by him or his position. And she was fiercely loyal to her family.

She proved it when she set both pen and pad down and leaned forward against the counter. "Look, Helen. I get it. You want to help Uncle Luke. But Catie worked for Mom. Mom helped her start her business. They were *friends*, and her friend is dead. You are not speaking to my mother."

I was so proud of her.

Except I really did want to speak with Sally.

I put a restraining hand on Helen, who might say heaven knew what in her pursuit of truth and justice. She was fired up about this case. She was just as upset as the rest of us, and she was channeling all those feelings into the pursuit of Catie's killer. I'd had to listen to her wildly theorize on the drive here. I'd talked her down from the serial killer angle, at least.

"When do you think might be a good time?" I asked.

When Helen would have spoken, pushed for an answer she wanted, I turned and presented her with the glare of death. I rarely used this particular evil genius skill, but when I had with my children, they'd complied.

"I'll just grab us a table," she said. "You can order for me."

I waited until she was seated. Since we'd been

early, there were only a few other people in the shop and no one behind me in line. I perused the menu, ordered food for both Helen and me, and then added a Himalayan cheese treat for Fairmont, who was waiting patiently in the car.

Food order complete, I said, "You know what Helen's like."

Annie tilted her head and presented me with an exaggerated oh-really look.

"Fine, I'm almost as bad. But if I didn't help them, Helen, Vanessa, and Georgie would likely drive off the edge of a cliff chasing after some bad guy."

"Fair point."

Annie tapped her pen on the counter. She was seventeen or eighteen, in her last year of high school, and caught in that in-between stage: not quite fully an adult, but no longer a girl.

Unlike Luke and Geraldine, Annie was of average height. Her hair was lighter, more a medium brown than brunette, and she had light hazel eyes. The eyes and height were Sally's, the hair her father's. Her figure was coltish, but that had more to do with an athletic bent and genetics than her age. If I had to guess, Annie would never be a curvy gal.

Her eyes narrowed. "What? You have a question you're dying to ask. Just go ahead."

"How well did you know her?"

She held up a finger, then left to deliver the order to the back, where I suspected her mom was hiding out and cooking. When she returned, I had my wallet out. Only after I'd paid did she say, "I knew her pretty well." She tipped her head. "As well as people knew Catie."

"How do you mean?"

She shrugged. "She was an on-the-surface friend, you know?"

"Superficial?" That hadn't been my impression of Catie.

"Not how you mean. Genuine, just hard to get to know. You never got through more than a few layers with Catie."

Annie was a clever kid. Not just good in school, but perceptive with people. I wasn't about to discount what she was saying, even if it didn't mesh well with my own impressions. But then I realized Annie's assessment did fit with one particular data point.

"Do you know where Catie moved here from?"

She gave me a knowing look. "No idea." She bit her lip. "Catie was good people. Nice to everyone, and Mom adored her, but she didn't share much of herself." But then she frowned. "I'm not saying it right. She'd do just about anything for her friends, and it sounds like I'm calling her shallow. It was just hard to get to know her on a really personal level."

"Thanks, Annie. I appreciate it. And I'm sorry."

Her face clouded for a second. "Yeah. I wasn't as close to her as Mom or Liam, but thanks."

"Let me know if you think your mom might want to talk about her. Helen and I just want to help find who did this."

Her expression sharpened, the sadness fading. "Because you don't think Uncle Luke can do his job?"

"Please. I know your Uncle Luke is an amazing sheriff. And *you* know Helen won't let it go." Nor would Georgie and Vanessa once they managed to finish their current project.

Annie looked like she was ready to deliver an epic eye roll, but then the bells on the door chimed. I was saved by Vince, the pizza boy.

I retreated with our drink order to the corner Helen had commandeered. Once I'd settled into my seat, I cast a glance over my shoulder at Vince looking lovesick as he ordered. "Just what White Sage needs, a love triangle."

Helen looked up from her phone. "Catie was in a love triangle? I didn't even know she was dating."

"Not Catie, Annie." But then that had me considering love and Catie. "Did Catie date?"

"I see where you're going with this. Love is one of the top motivators for murder."

"I beg to disagree. Love doesn't motivate murder.

Perhaps spoiled, twisted love does. Love that's gone wrong. Or some of the less savory side effects of love."

Helen ticked them off on her fingers. "Jealousy, lust, infidelity... I do see your point about spoiled love. Healthy relationships might have jealousy, but not to a degree sufficient to motivate murder."

I wrinkled my nose. "I feel like we should be leaving the motive part to Georgie and Vanessa."

"Nonsense. It's money, love—or, as you've pointed out, spoiled love—sex, or secrets."

Georgie had been the one to point out not so long ago that in a small town, secrets were few and far between, but if they *did* exist, the owners of those secrets could be vicious in their guarding of them.

She'd been right on the money.

"Don't forget revenge." That had been the motivator in another Sleuthing Granny Gang case.

Helen tilted her head as she considered that. "I feel like that ties in with your spoiled love theory. It's a nice umbrella motive."

Annie appeared and thunked our sandwiches down on the table. "You two keep your voices down. This is a nice place. We don't need the kind of ambiance that murder meetings create."

First, I wanted to know how she knew that we called our get-togethers "murder meetings."

Second, she was doing an excellent job of channeling her mother.

Which she must have realized, because she rolled her eyes. "I need to get out of here. College can't come too soon."

Once she'd returned to the counter, I said in a voice just barely above a whisper, "We need to find out more about Catie, starting with where she came from and why Luke was guarding that information like it's top secret."

Helen's eyes widened. "Say what?"

I might have forgotten to mention that to the gang—on purpose. His reaction had been odd, and while Luke didn't confide information that wasn't his to share, if he did, I would protect it. I wouldn't use our relationship to further the SGG's goals.

He hadn't told me anything, but he obliquely had by his very reaction. I felt like I'd just been disloyal, which I hadn't been, but I wasn't elaborating.

"Fine. Don't tell me." She attacked her sandwich with all the vigor of a woman who hadn't just eaten an everything bagel with Swiss cheese and ham less than an hour ago.

We ate in silence—me enjoying my chicken avocado panini, Helen her roast beef—until Helen finished. I still had half a sandwich left when she smacked the table and said, "Witness protection."

I smiled. I couldn't help it. Witness protection?

Really?

"Laugh if you like, but it's a real thing."

"Oh, I believe that witness protection exists. I don't believe that Catie was a part of it." What would be the odds of that?

Helen gave that some thought then finally conceded, "I suppose if she was then there would be someone else on the case. The FBI or US Marshals or whoever wouldn't let Luke investigate the murder."

"Probably not." Except... As far-fetched as Helen's witness protection theory might be—I placed it in the realm of her serial killer theories—there was a tiny kernel of possibility in it.

Witness protection was all about hiding witnesses from harm so they could testify, and they did that by reinventing the witness as a new person. But you didn't need to be in witness protection to reinvent yourself.

I knew that intimately. I'd reinvented myself when I moved to White Sage. I'd even changed my name. I'd abandoned my ex's name and assumed my maiden name, like many divorced women, but what was to keep a person from simply choosing another name?

The SGG had encountered another victim who'd done that—he'd simply been very open about it.

"I can see the wheels turning. What are you

thinking?"

I glanced at the second half of my sandwich. "I'm thinking I should finish my sandwich, so that Fairmont can get home and sleep the afternoon away on the sofa instead of on his dog bed in the back of the Grand Cherokee."

"Go on, then. Nothing's stopping you." She tapped her finger on the table. "Except I was thinking we'd make a stop first."

I raised my eyebrows. We could. Fairmont loved the car, and since October had been fairly cool so far, it wasn't too warm for him. But I was exhausted. I wanted a nap. Today had been an emotional roller coaster.

Then again... My computer was at home. I'd turned off the email notifications to my phone ages ago, and even removed the app. I could check my email using the web browser on my cell, but I never did. It was unwieldy to type responses, and nothing in my inbox was that important. Usually.

But once I was home, I'd check my email. Just in case one of the emails I'd sent had already borne fruit.

"Yes, we can make time for another stop."

"Good." She smiled, but it was grim. "I hope you're craving something sweet."

The last few bites of my panini lost their appeal. I pushed the plate aside.

Walking into Catie's Cupcakery, knowing Catie wouldn't be there, knowing what had happened to her—

"They're open. I checked before we came in."

I nodded, because I had too. Sally's was only two doors away. It had been impossible not to look as I'd parked in front of both buildings.

"At least we know that it didn't happen there." Helen blinked. "She wouldn't have wanted—"

I knew what she was going to say. That Catie wouldn't have wanted something so terrible to blight her beautiful shop.

"Sorry." Helen shook her head.

"No, you're right. She loved that shop. She wouldn't have wanted anything bad to happen there."

Still, it was a little shocking they hadn't closed for the day, and that was enough to spark my curiosity and chase away any reservations I had about crossing the threshold.

Money, love, sex, secrets, or revenge. That was our motive list.

Who inherited the shop? Did any of Catie's employees know the secrets of Catie's past or her love life?

A tiny shop with a tight-knit group of employees? Someone there would know Catie's secrets, or perhaps have a motive of their own.

8

No way was there a motive for murder among this crowd.

The moment Helen and I stepped inside the shop, we realized why they'd remained open. The three employees—Steph, the part-time baker and dog treat maker; Angela, the full-time cashier, frosting expert, and backup baker; and Miles, the part-time cashier—were giving away the day's stock in exchange for donations to Catie's funeral fund.

My eyes burned with an excess of emotion, and I just wanted this day to be over.

But these people who cared about Catie had gathered in her shop to do the thing she'd loved—provide the community with treats so sweet they made you smile—and to provide for Catie.

I loved White Sage.

If they didn't get enough donations to cover her funeral, I'd be shocked. The store wasn't full, but it was bustling. And yes, some of the people in attendance were there for gossip, but most were there because Catie had brightened their lives.

Steph saw us at the door and lifted a hand in greeting. Then she approached and hugged us, first Helen and then me. She was thin and felt fragile as I returned her hug. When she stepped back, I saw that her eyes were red-rimmed and bloodshot. "Thanks for stopping by. We appreciate the support."

Helen was already reaching for her purse and pulling her checkbook out. While many of White Sage's residents were entrepreneurial, working two or even three side hustles in addition to a full-time job, I knew that Helen had settled in White Sage after both she and her husband had retired from successful careers. She, unlike Georgie and Vanessa, had entered retirement well situated.

While Helen wrote a check, I expressed my sympathies.

Helen handed the check to Steph, then asked, "Do you know what will happen with the shop? It's become such a fixture in such a short time."

"I'm not sure. I suppose it depends on what the will says." Steph lifted the now-folded check. "Thank you, Helen."

I avoided Helen's gaze, because I knew she was

thinking exactly what I was: what twenty-something had a will?

Instead, I focused all of my attention on Steph and said, "I don't have my checkbook with me, but I'd like to contribute. How should I do that?"

She told me that I could drop the check with Angela any time over the next few days, since she'd be manning the shop until everything was sorted. "We want to stay open for the sake of the business. It barely runs at a profit, and it might not recover from a lengthy closure."

The fact that Catie's Cupcakes had employed Catie in addition to one full-time and two part-time employees *and* made a profit, however small, so early after the business's formation was astounding. Even taking into account the amazing product, Catie's endless energy, and the draw of her warm personality, it was still noteworthy.

Helen stepped into the silence. "I suppose Saturday is one of your biggest days." Tomorrow was Saturday.

Angela, who'd been busy filling boxes with cupcakes when we'd entered the store, joined us. "It is. We're hoping by the end of the day tomorrow to have enough to cover Catie's funeral expenses. She doesn't have any family besides us to handle the arrangements, and the funeral will need to be handled long before the estate is settled."

Angela, unlike Steph, didn't look like she'd been crying. In fact, she looked far from tears. Her face was full of fierce determination. I could practically hear her thoughts: focus on the goal; raise money for the funeral.

People expressed grief in many ways, and I suspected that Angela wouldn't be having a good, long cry until Catie's funeral was over, her business affairs sorted, and there was nothing left to do but let the sadness creep in.

Helen, never one to let a sensitive situation dissuade her from asking questions, said, "If the store is barely in the black, how are you able to give away all of these cupcakes, cookies, and candies today?"

Angela shot Steph what appeared to be a disapproving look. Perhaps because she'd revealed the state of the books? But she answered Helen's question. "We've all waived our wages for the week. We didn't think it was right to take money from the business right now."

"Especially since we might not technically have the authority," Steph said. "Until we hear from Catie's attorney, we don't know who actually owns the business."

"That's awkward, given the circumstances." I wasn't intimately familiar with the workings of wills, but I knew whose I was included in.

My parents and my ex both had provisions in their wills for me. My parents because I would inherit the bulk of their estate, and my ex because I was the trustee of my children's trust accounts.

Wasn't it typical to inform the beneficiary of a will of one's inclusion? And if Catie had done so, then either one of her employees was keeping secrets, or Catie had friends and family that her cupcake shop family was unaware of.

"It's only awkward because the attorney who drafted the will took a three-day weekend, starting last night," Angela said. Her lips pinched. "Miles called this morning and caught his secretary. She said he's officially unplugged."

Angela did not approve of unplugging, clearly.

I couldn't really blame her. It seemed unwise as an estate lawyer to be completely unreachable. Or was it? He was technically only out one business day, and again, who didn't inform the beneficiaries of their will that they were being included?

I had no frame of reference for normal behavior, only my own experiences to go by. But now I had so many questions. Why did such a young woman with no children have a will? While it was a wise choice, especially as a business owner, I suspected it was also an unusual one. And having created a will, why didn't anyone know who inherited the business?

And there was the niggling thought that as fabulous as Catie had been, it was still noteworthy that she'd gotten her business—one with an expensive professional kitchen, Main Street rent, and a handful of employees—off the ground and running in the black in only a few short months.

The chimes on the door interrupted the string of questions flowing through my mind. All thoughts of wills and account ledgers disappeared as Bubba Charleston entered the shop.

Bubba Charleston, aka Police Chief Charleston, aka the other arm of the law in White Sage. I couldn't help wondering if, just maybe, whatever Luke had been hesitant to disclose about Catie's past was also a nugget of knowledge that had been shared with the chief.

While Helen and Geraldine had both been underwhelmed by Chief Charleston's competence, I hadn't found the same to be true.

The man had a miniscule budget, and he focused on the things he could most directly impact: safe driving, clean streets, and keeping the townsfolk sober and civil on a day-to-day basis. Serious crime might be outside his realm of expertise, but he also knew it. That was why the chief ceded jurisdiction to the county and its former Austin PD homicide detective sheriff when more serious crimes cropped up inside White Sage city limits.

Except when that sheriff was out of town at a

bachelor party in New Orleans. And when that had happened, the chief had stepped up.

His willingness to delegate without ego and his ability to competently step in when necessary put Bubba Charleston on my to-be-admired list.

He also happened to have a romantic history with my boyfriend's mom and was a seriously nice guy, not to mention good looking for an older man. I really liked Bubba Charleston.

"Hi, chief." I summoned a genuine smile.

"Zella, Helen." He inclined his head. Not exactly the warmest of greetings, but then, he'd probably been warned by Luke that the SGG was already underfoot. "Angela, Stephanie, I'm sorry for your loss. Everyone thought very highly of Catie. This will be a difficult time for the community. We, White Sage PD, appreciate everything you're doing here."

A flash of some strong emotion lit Steph's eyes. Was she angry with the chief? What beef could she have with Bubba Charleston?

He held out an envelope. "This is for your collection, from Charlene, Gary, Meg, and me."

He'd listed the entirety of the White Sage police force. Teeny-tiny budgets meant teeny-tiny departments. And Meg wasn't even working now; she was on maternity leave. So WSPD was down to Charlene, Greg, and the chief.

Miles appeared at the chief's elbow with a box.

"Thanks for the donation, chief. A box of lemon basil blueberry cupcakes for you and the staff. These are WSPD's favorite, right?"

"Yes, thank you, Miles." Bubba turned to Angela. "You'll let us know if there's anything we can do for you?"

"Yes, we'll do that," Angela replied.

But really, what could Chief Charleston do? What could any of us do?

Except find the killer.

When the chief left, Helen and I followed on his heels.

Once we were outside and a few feet beyond view of the shop's front door, the chief stopped abruptly and turned to us. "No."

"We didn't say a word. Really, Bubba Charleston." Helen infused his full name with all the judgment of a Southern woman full-naming a child. "You can be downright unfriendly at times."

"If it means I save myself from being grilled on the Main Street sidewalk, I'm all right with unfriendly." He gave me an apologetic look.

I ignored that look, because I was definitely intent on grilling him now that he'd implicitly revealed he had useful information. Why else would he be avoiding Helen and me? Contrary to Helen's comment, Bubba Charleston was an outgoing, friendly man.

I took a stab in the dark. "Where did Catie move here from, chief?"

"Outside the state, I believe."

Which was more of an answer than anyone else had. I suspected he knew Catie Smithart's previous address and much more.

"Arkansas?"

"I'm not sure."

"New Mexico?"

He shifted his weight and gave me the look.

"Louisiana?"

"Why do you want to know?" he asked.

Did that mean Louisiana was the right answer? Probably not. Heck, she might not even be from out of state. Much as Helen and Geraldine thought Bubba was a fool, the man absolutely was not.

"We want to know," Helen replied, "because no one seems to know, and that's hinky."

"Hinky? Maybe she's a private person." He closed his eyes for a beat. "Maybe she *was* a private person. Don't pry, Helen. Luke has this well in hand. Please. Both of you. Stay away from this. It's a nasty business."

Bubba Charleston sounded like he knew something. That, or he'd heard about Catie's injuries.

Her extensive injuries. I didn't want to dwell on the image, but it wasn't like I could wash it away. Whoever had hurt her hadn't stopped with one blow. I was fairly certain she'd been stabbed, and more than once.

I looked away, toward Main Street. Away from this conversation and my memories.

It took me a few seconds to focus on what was directly in front of me, but when I did, I couldn't resist a grin.

"Chief Charleston?"

"I can't help you. Actually, I can help you—by not speaking about this case. Period."

I bit my lip. "Uh-huh. Chief, I think your puppy is eating your seat belt."

That got his attention. He looked up and hollered, "Turbo!"

Wide, tawny eyes stared back at him...and he still had the seat belt trapped in his cute puppy jaws. The edge was frayed and damp.

The cruiser was city property, and as such, not a late model. (No budget for new vehicles.) But up until the addition of Turbo, it had been in very good condition.

Bubba hustled around to the passenger side and opened the door. He attached Turbo's leash, then lifted him out of the car and set him on the ground. "Ladies, meet Turbo. Turbo, say hello."

The adorable troublemaking tripod German shorthaired pointer promptly sat.

"Please pet him. We've been working on this, and if you don't pet him—"

Too late. Turbo sprang into the air and planted his single left front paw firmly on my chest.

Bubba walked away, bringing Turbo with him. "Apologies. He's a work in progress."

"Aren't we all," Helen murmured. Then again, she could be magnanimous. She hadn't just suffered the indignity of a paw to the right boob.

I discreetly rubbed the offended area while the chief knelt down and petted the now-sitting Turbo.

"All right. Let's try this one more time." I eyed the chief's low position. "I assume if I'm down there, he's not up here." I indicated my face and chest.

Bubba chuckled. "Correct, but you don't have to play the game. Another month or two and we should have this particular quirk of his sorted out."

I thought of Fairmont, asleep in the back of my Jeep. Someone had taught him to sit nicely for human attention. And potty-trained him. Taught him to love car rides, walk nicely on a leash—and find dead people. Someone out in the world loved Fairmont just as Bubba Charleston so clearly adored Turbo.

I walked purposefully toward the puppy. I swore to myself when I sent those emails that I wouldn't borrow trouble. That I'd send the emails and then wouldn't worry until I received an actual reply.

A reply that might possibly be waiting for me in my inbox right now.

I knelt quickly, before Turbo's two seconds of patience expired, and petted him thoroughly. When his excitement overcame his ability to plant his rear on the ground, I stood up and walked away.

"You've done this before," Bubba said.

"Only with children," I replied wryly. "I assume the same basic principles apply. Fairmont was a perfect gentleman from the moment I adopted him."

Helen placed her hand on my back. It was a supportive gesture, so some of my stress must be showing.

"Is Fairmont all right?" Bubba asked. He looked around, probably for my Jeep.

"He's fine. He's asleep in the car." I looked over my shoulder to find that Fairmont was not asleep. He was watching us through the window of the driver's seat.

When left to his own devices in the car, he invariably migrated to the driver's seat, even though the entire back of the Grand Cherokee was set up as his own home away from home, with a fluffy dog bed and blankets.

"We've been a little longer than planned," I said, feeling guilty for leaving him stranded in the car for so long.

As we watched, he stretched and yawned.

"I don't think he's very concerned about it," Bubba commented. "We should introduce these two. Soon, but not today."

No, not today.

He picked up Turbo to put him in the car, and I wished I was faster with my cell camera. At six foot four or five, Bubba Charleston was a big man, and he kept himself fit. Turbo couldn't have been more than five or six months old. Not a young puppy, but still adorably puppylike.

And for the moment he cradled the pup in his arms, Bubba and Turbo were just about swoon-worthy.

Helen poked me hard in the side. "Quit making eyes at Bubba Charleston. You have a boyfriend."

Did I? I wasn't so sure after our conversation last night. I had a friend in Luke, but we'd have to wait to see if the other parts of our relationship weathered any future interaction—or lack thereof—with my offspring.

But either way, objectively noticing a man's attractiveness was not "making eyes" at him. I had absolutely no romantic interest in Bubba Charleston.

I waved goodbye to the chief. "I definitely have romance on my mind." When Helen poked me harder, I turned to her with a grin. "Geraldine and Bubba's romance, Helen."

"There is no Geraldine and Bubba." She scowled as she rounded the front of the Grand Cherokee. "I don't understand why you're so charitable when it comes to that man. He's a menace with a shiny badge."

After greeting Fairmont with chin scratches and ear rubs, I pointed to the rear of the SUV. He hopped into the back without hesitation.

"Chief Charleston isn't a menace, and you know it."

Where was all of this animosity coming from? Helen wasn't as rabid in her criticism of the chief as Geraldine, but she wasn't his biggest fan.

"Humph." Helen only relaxed when Fairmont nudged her shoulder, begging for pets. She scratched him behind the ears.

"Helen, the man is the chief of police. White Sage may be tiny, but he still runs the police force. Very competently, I might add." I waited for a few cars to pass before backing out.

As I pulled forward, I caught a glimpse of her in my peripheral vision. She had the look of a woman dying to spill a juicy tale but held back by...something.

Usually, she was less than complimentary of the chief. Today, on the heels of my proposed match-making, her dissatisfaction had been amplified to as-yet-unseen heights. Wild guess, there was a connection there.

I headed toward Helen's house, which was basically heading home, because she only lived a few streets away from me. "Does your poor opinion have something to do with Geraldine?"

She tipped her head slightly.

I interpreted that to mean warm, but not hot. If not Geraldine, then... "Luke?"

"Yes." She paused, then said, "You know Luke and I have our differences."

A snort escaped before I could stop it. "More like you and May were forever stepping on his investigative toes. He had to breathe a huge sigh of relief when your last sleuthing buddy moved away to live closer to her son. Then again, I suppose the SGG is worse."

Instead of one gang member egging her on, now she had two and half. I was the half, because I was one part support and one part "no, you may not do that."

"Hmm."

"Helen. He's just worried you'll commit an actual crime." My tone lost its teasing note as I added, "Or suffer a head injury, maybe."

I wasn't ashamed to harp on her hospitalization for a concussion. Not if it kept her from taking so many risks.

"There might be some truth to that." She waved her hand as if her past near-criminal acts and head wound were of no significance. "The important thing is that he's a good man, and he didn't deserve to grow up without a father."

I almost missed the turn into our neighborhood, because...what?

What did Chief Charleston have to do with Luke's fatherless— "Oh." The chief had said he and Geraldine had been high school sweethearts, that they'd even dated in college.

But Bubba couldn't be Luke's father, because... "Geraldine married another man."

I parked in Helen's drive then turned to her. She arched an eyebrow.

"Right. I do understand biology. But marrying one man while carrying another's baby doesn't seem very like the Geraldine I know." I narrowed my eyes. "Not that I'm saying that's wrong. Neither of us knows the circumstances of her marriage or anything about her life back then, so we shouldn't judge."

Helen smiled back at me innocently. "I'm not judging Geraldine McCord. I'm judging that snake of a cop. You've seen the tension between Bubba and Geraldine, and Luke looks like him."

There was a *passing* resemblance. They were

both tall, athletic, attractive men with dark hair and light eyes. Beyond that? I sighed. Maybe.

"I don't know, Helen. Should you say such things without any real proof?" Within seconds, I conjured several scenarios to explain the discord between Geraldine and the chief, none of which involved Luke's parentage.

Besides, the parentage of her child was a private matter between Geraldine and the chief. Speculation seemed invasive and unkind.

She lifted her chin. "I know what I know."

"Except you don't really." I turned to look at Fairmont, curled up on his bed. He didn't look in desperate need of a potty break, and my house was just around the corner. "Go on your afternoon walk, fix a snack, do what you do, but don't do any investigating without calling me first."

She pointed a finger at me. "I could say the same to you."

I hadn't a clue what she was talking about. I was going home to take a nap.

After I checked my email.

9

N ot a single reply to the eight emails I'd sent this morning waited in my inbox.

Which meant that I'd had a glorious late afternoon nap.

A run might have been a better stress reliever, and I knew Fairmont always enjoyed a jog around the neighborhood, but I'd been so very tired.

As always, Fairmont had been happy to keep me company whatever my chosen activity. I stretched under the weight of my down duvet, and he shifted at my feet.

With a glance at the window, I found it significantly darker than when we'd lain down to rest. The days were getting shorter, though, so I wasn't sure how long I'd slept.

I hunted around in the covers for my cell phone.

Once I found it, I discovered it was past eight o'clock, and I'd missed a few text messages.

Good thing I hadn't just slept on through the night. This late in the evening, that was always a possibility. As it was, I felt groggy rather than refreshed and had regrets about skipping the run.

Once my feet were firmly planted on the floor, I looked at the messages again. One stood out, since it was sent from a number that wasn't programmed in my phone.

Can we talk? Miles

Miles. From Catie's shop. He'd sent it about a half hour ago.

Instead of texting him back, I called.

"Hey," he answered on the first ring. "I hope you don't think this is weird, but I'm on your porch right now."

Definitely weird. Maybe it was the Southern in me or maybe I was too tired to think straight, but I replied, "No problem."

"If it helps, I have cupcakes and a dog chew for Fairmont."

Since I'd forgotten to give him the chew I'd bought at Sally's earlier, I was pretty sure Fairmont would be full of ecstatic dog joy to receive one now. And my empty stomach wasn't sad about the cupcakes.

Still groggy, I replied, "Thank you. Give me just a few minutes to get myself together."

Seven minutes later, Fairmont had taken a quick potty break while I'd freshened up in the bathroom. If a person shows up on your doorstep uninvited, they can wait five minutes for brushed hair, a makeup touchup, and more appropriate clothing than PJ bottoms and a tank top with no bra.

When I napped, I liked to go all out. What was the point otherwise?

I opened the door to a white pastry box extended by a man wearing his medium brown hair in a tidy bun and an apologetic expression on his face. "Forgive me?"

At least he realized that showing up basically unannounced wasn't good form. I snatched the box from his hands. "Forgiven."

I waited for him to explain why he was here.

He peered over his shoulder. "Uh, any chance we can chat inside?"

That wasn't suspicious. Not at all. I considered whether I should maybe text someone before I let him in, but then I looked at him, standing on my porch, and he seemed more embarrassed than anything else.

And who would I text? Anyone who came to mind would tell me to either kick him off my porch or wait until reinforcements arrived. And I didn't want him to leave. I was curious.

After what was likely an awkwardly long period of time, I ushered him inside.

He stooped to pet Fairmont before following me into the kitchen. An action I found oddly reassuring. "Can I give him the chew I brought?"

I eyed the chew that looked exactly like all the others made by Steff, then said, "Sure. Thanks for thinking of him."

I hunted around in the cupboard for my one herbal tea, the apple spice, and displayed it for Miles' approval. "This is it for caffeine-free options. Unless you'd prefer coffee? It's a little late, but if you like...?"

When he murmured his agreement to the caffeine-free option, I set about filling my electric kettle and retrieving plates.

Fairmont was already planted on his dog bed, gnawing on his cheesy treat. He had the yellow stick clutched firmly between his two front paws and his little tail was wagging with barely suppressed joy.

My chest tightened. I loved him so much.

But I wasn't borrowing trouble. I was waiting to hear back. I wasn't having a panic attack in my kitchen over the as-yet-unknown future of my pet.

I turned back to the box Miles had brought. Cupcakes. I had cupcakes. I popped open the pastry box to find an assortment of six. "Which would you like?"

"I like them all. One of the perks of working part-time at the Cupcakery, I get to take home as many day-olds as I like." He sat down at the card table still serving duty as my kitchen table.

The lemon basil blueberry that the chief and Charlene liked so much made its way onto my plate, and I sacrificed the chocolate explosion—a chocolate cupcake with dark chocolate chips and creamy chocolate frosting—to Miles. He was young. He could handle the thousand-plus calories packed into that one sinfully delicious treat.

With both of us settled, food and drink at our fingertips, I expected Miles to get to the point of his text.

He didn't. He ate his cupcake. Drank his tea. Twiddled his thumbs. He *figuratively* twiddled his thumbs; he *actually* sat across from me looking extremely uncomfortable.

"I'm never one to decline hand-delivered treats, but I don't think that's the only reason you stopped by."

"No." His dark eyes met mine, and I could see the conflict there. "Catie's is a small shop. And you know we haven't been open very long?"

"Yes." Everyone knew everything about the shops on Main Street. White Sage was the county seat to a county of twenty thousand, but the town itself was only around five thousand people. It would be hard *not* to know about every new venture, especially those that opened on the main drag in town.

"You'd never guess how new the business is from how tight we all are. Were."

Ah. Now I could see the problem. "If you have information that you think could help solve Catie's murder, you should tell Luke. He's not going to run around accusing innocent people. He'll investigate and follow up leads responsibly."

"Yeah." Miles didn't look happy with my response. Then he shot me a hopeful puppy-dog look. "But can't I just tell you, and you can decide if it's important?"

I set my mug down and looked at him. Maybe because he excelled at growing facial hair, maybe because he was tall, maybe because he came across as a serious guy, but I'd assumed Miles was well into his twenties.

Now, on closer inspection, I'd place him closer to twenty than to twenty-nine.

"Where do you work, Miles? Besides Catie's, I mean."

His eyes brightened. "I'm an artist, and I do a little graphic design. I just got my first cover art gig." He grinned, all teeth and excitement. "Vanessa put me in touch with an author who was looking for some art like mine."

"I hope it works out." I sipped my tea as I considered my options. Send him to Luke and risk him walking out of my house with whatever information he had and him not following up with Luke or anyone else.

Or listen.

I could always send him straight to Luke if it was something important or tell Luke myself.

Miles leaned back in his chair, a smudge of chocolate on his lip making him look even younger than he was.

"All right, Miles. What's on your mind?"

"It's all gonna come out anyway. And I don't think it means anything. Not like I think this has anything to do with what happened to Catie. Not really."

But it might, or he wouldn't be here. I understood where he was coming from. No one wanted to believe that the people closest to us—our friends, our family, our loved ones—were capable of unkind acts. Certainly, we didn't want to believe them capable of violence.

But people we loved let us down.

They lied to us.

They betrayed wedding vows.

They put their own wants first, even when it was harmful to the ones they loved.

Sometimes those acts destroyed our love, like my own for my ex-husband. It had been a bright and shining thing inside me. But over time, those unkind acts had whittled it away to nothing.

Sometimes those ungenerous acts were simply a blip on the radar. Like my children's current obsession with their mother remaining free of romantic entanglements.

But either way, the reality was that people didn't always act as we hoped they would.

"Whatever it is, it's weighing on you."

He nodded slowly. "Yeah. I know what's in the will. I know who inherits the Cupcakery."

"Okay." This didn't seem like such a pivotal piece of information to me. The Cupcakery was a great idea, and it had potential, but actual monetary value? The business had to still be carrying debt at this point.

"So, you know, that's like a motive, right?" he asked, looking worried.

"Maybe? But it can't be worth much. The equipment is expensive but probably not paid off for three to five years. The brand and client list might—"

"No, you don't understand. Catie bought the equipment outright—and the shop. Catie's Cupcakery has been running in the black because there's no rent, no debt maintenance for the professional kitchen upgrade or for the equipment."

"Oh." My stomach sank, because yes, that might be motive.

I knew how much property sold for on Main Street. There were only so many shops on that small strip, and the town had been experiencing growth as its infrastructure had improved. Stable internet alone had propelled growth in White Sage, as Austinites fled expensive housing and the rising costs of living there.

And Catie's wasn't just the shop; there was an apartment above where she'd lived. The shop, the apartment, the renovations she'd made to improve the property, the equipment, the client list, the branding...

Would someone kill for all of that?

Many people had killed for less.

But would *these* people kill for ownership of Catie's Cupcakery?

"Miles, who inherits Catie's?"

He blinked. "Angela. But I really don't think she'd ever want to hurt Catie. I don't think she could."

There was one problem with the will's contents as motive for murder. "Do you think Angela knows Catie included her in the will?"

"Yeah. That's how I know. I heard her and Catie

talking about it. About how Catie was going to see her lawyer in Austin that week and she was going to make sure that Angela got the shop in her will."

Which raised a few questions, not least of which was—why hadn't Angela stepped up and said the shop was hers? It was hardly the time and place to tell clients, but even Steph hadn't known.

In fact, Steph had acted as if the entire staff—her, Angela, and Miles—weren't certain of the shop's ownership and wouldn't be until the estate attorney had been reached.

Catie's visit to an attorney in Austin raised another question. "Is that where Catie's from? Austin?"

"No, she's not. I mean, I don't *know* that, but I don't think so." Miles shrugged. "She went there for work stuff. Anything she couldn't get locally or shipped at a reasonable rate to the store, she drove into Austin to fetch."

"Things like flour and sugar and eggs?"

"Oh, no. We get that all locally. Like, really local. So, the eggs we use? They're from the Hen Coop, a bunch of White Sage locals who banded together so they could find a bigger market for their eggs. And a lot of the specialty ingredients are local, as well. The lavender, for example, is from a farm that's about twenty miles down the road. Cool, right? Catie liked to incorporate super-local ingredients as much as possible." He scrubbed his hands across his face. "Man, I'm gonna miss her."

I quietly agreed that we all would.

Almost everyone. Someone had obviously wanted her gone.

A shiver went up my spine. White Sage was generally a very welcoming place—except when it wasn't. I hadn't told Luke or the SGG about any of the nasty notes I'd received in the past few weeks. All of them had the same theme. I wasn't welcome here, and I needed to leave.

Not so very long ago, I'd found a dead grackle on my back porch along with a note telling me to get out of town. The notes that had followed hadn't included any more dead birds, thank goodness.

"Zella?" Miles said, looking at me curiously. "What do you think?"

It took me a second to orient myself to the current problem. This wasn't the time to dwell on nasty notes or ambiguous threats.

There was a very real, very current threat at large.

Miles leaned forward, looking anxious. "Do you think it's important? Because I really don't think Angela could hurt anyone, especially not Catie. She really appreciated Catie giving her a second chance."

My ears perked up at that. "A second chance?"

"Yeah. You know, Angela and I are both kinda

White Sage losers." He rolled his eyes. "As if we care about that. The world is a bigger place than White Sage. But when you're looking for work here, it can be hard to counter that kind of label."

I didn't ask what made Miles a White Sage loser. It wouldn't shock me if his attempt to pay his bills with his art had landed him in that category. The internet might be solid here, but that was a newer development. And the idea of virtual work and creative gigs as a means of income was still a fairly new one to the locals.

They'd catch on quickly—this town knew how to hustle—but it was natural for there to be some lag.

"What about Angela's history made her unattractive as an employee?" From what I'd seen, she was hardworking and no-nonsense.

Miles shrugged. His go-to, I was learning, when he was uncomfortable with what he was sharing. "This is the first job where she's fit in. She hasn't always gotten along with management or sometimes even the customers. But at the shop, she's been really cool to work with. And I've only ever seen her be really nice to customers. I think she's happy there."

"Yeah, I understand."

We all searched until we found our place, in work and in relationships. Angela had kept trying, and I was happy for her that she'd landed somewhere she felt she belonged. But what if that sense of belonging had been jeopardized?

Now that she'd finally found work—and, from the way Miles talked about their little group, a kind of second family—what would she do to keep that?

"Do you know if Angela and Catie had any disagreements recently?"

"No. I mean, I can't be sure, but they seemed solid to me. Angela worked really hard. She and Catie both wanted the same thing: for the shop to be successful."

"Okay." I clutched my warm mug in my hand and glanced at Fairmont. He'd fallen asleep with the chew clutched between his front legs.

"You think I should tell Luke."

I hadn't gotten so far in my thoughts, but it was pretty clear he should. "I do."

The flare of panic on Miles' face surprised me.

Luke wasn't intimidating. He didn't abuse his position. Luke McCord was the very definition of community policing. He knew and loved the town and its residents. He did his best for the people of Sage County.

"Can you tell him for me?" Miles pleaded with his sad puppy-dog eyes.

My son Mark had mastered that particular look almost before he could walk, so I was well equipped to resist. "I think it would be better coming directly from you."

He shook his head. "I can't."

He'd gone all pale.

"Miles." I gave him my best disapproving mother look. "Why exactly do you not want to speak directly with Luke?"

"It's nothing to do with this. I swear." His knee bounced nervously. "I just can't look him in the eye without... I just can't."

"You're going to tell me what you've done." Because he had almost certainly committed an illegal act. The boy—young man—was terrified Luke would find him out. When he didn't immediately spill his guts, I said, very firmly, "Now."

He groaned. "You know Megan?"

I vaguely knew Megan. Not to be confused with Meg. Meg was the WSPD employee I'd never met who was currently on maternity leave. Megan was younger, probably around Miles' age. "I know who she is."

"We went to high school together. She has a kid brother, Matthew, and he is seriously talented."

I had a vague recollection of a Matthew who had periodical difficulties with Bubba Charleston due to his habit of spray-painting his "art" all over town.

"Miles Burford. You have not been encouraging that child to deface property, have you?"

His knee bounced faster. I took that to mean, at the very least, yes.

Miles was an artist himself. Was he mentoring this Matthew child?

"How old is he?"

His knee slowed down. "Sixteen. He's almost old enough to vote."

Almost old enough to... "Miles, you have got to be kidding me."

He groaned again. "And I might have helped him improve his technique...a little."

I rubbed my forehead. "So you've been defacing property, encouraging illegal behavior in a minor, and now you're worried about spilling the beans to Luke."

"What?" He frowned. "I'm spilling no beans. My beans are locked up tight. I would never get Matthew in any trouble, and there's no way I'm taking any flack for the improvements we made to the old Carson warehouse."

"Oh." I knew exactly what he was talking about. "That is a very pretty mural."

"Right? We're really good together."

"You're committing illegal acts together."

"And improving the community. That place hasn't been anything but an eyesore for years. And now it's"—he grinned and then turned my own words back on me—"pretty."

Probably not his preferred adjective. And it was rawer and bolder than a "pretty" picture, but I couldn't deny I enjoyed that particular piece.

"All right. Here's the issue. You work at Catie's and the owner has been murdered. Luke is going to interview you."

"He already did, but I was pretty upset and couldn't say much."

"Right. He'll be back when you're not in a state of shock for a more complete statement." Miles sank down in the chair, so I continued, "But—I'll speak to him."

"Thank you!"

I held up a finger. "About the vandalism."

"I don't appreciate that word."

"Then you shouldn't vandalize property." When he would have protested, I interrupted him. "Shush. I'll tell him, on the quiet, about your nefarious illegal activities and also that you'll be coming to speak with him to give him a second statement."

He pulled a little-boy pouty face.

I wagged a finger at him. "That won't work with me. I have a son who makes you look like an amateur."

He huffed out a breath. "Fine, but if I end up in the slammer because I can't pay the fines and then become a career criminal, you should definitely feel bad."

Which made me laugh. Because how adorable was he? "I can't make any promises, but you do realize that Luke is investigating a murder. That's his priority right now."

And if I had any influence at all with that man, I'd try to encourage him not to make a fuss about a little graffiti, especially the kind that beautified nasty abandoned buildings.

"Ugh. All right, I'll call him. I mean, I knew I'd have to talk to him; I was just worried that I'd look all guilty, and he'd think I'd done something worse. You know?"

I did know. "So you'll call him and set up an appointment."

"Right." He moved to stand up.

"Sit," I said in my firm, you-will-obey-your-mother voice.

He sat.

"You'll call now, thank you very much."

He squinted warily at me. It was a look straight out of the teenage boy handbook. Maybe I'd overestimated. Maybe Miles was only eighteen or nineteen.

"I feel kinda bad for your kids," he said as he started to dial. "Wait a sec. I don't have to call the main line. You probably have Luke's cell number, right?"

I rolled my eyes and grabbed his phone. As if it

was some great coup for him to get Luke's number out of me. If he was calling to set up an appointment, I'd gladly give it to him.

"Hey, Sheriff McCord. It's Miles Burford. I'm at Zella's house, and— No, she's fine." He grinned at me, but then all humor faded. "Yeah, about that. I was hoping I could set up a time to give you my statement. Tomorrow morning?"

He looked at me, and I nodded. I'd be sure to chat with Luke before then.

"Yeah, tomorrow at nine is great." Although his tone said it really wasn't. "Um, yeah, sure."

He handed the phone to me.

"Hi, Luke."

"You have something you need to tell me?" The deep tones of his familiar voice slid straight from my ear to my heart.

I missed him. I'd seen him this morning, and we hadn't left things on the best of terms last night, and yet I missed him.

"I do. Have you eaten dinner?"

"It's almost nine. Unlike some people, I remember to feed myself most days."

I glanced at the box of cupcakes. I still had four left. "I do too, most days. How about some cupcakes?"

"You offering to come over?"

"I'm asking if I can." There was a difference

between the two, and we both knew it. Time for me to make a few concessions, because it seemed it was usually Luke doing the bending.

"I'd love to see you." He hesitated. "But I'm going through some statements, so I don't have a lot of time."

Fair enough. The man was in the middle of a murder investigation. "See you shortly. As soon as I kick out Miles and wake up Fairmont."

"That sounds great. And Zella? Thank you." Then he hung up.

Another reason I adored this man. He noticed all the little things. I'd bent a little, acknowledged the fact that I was missing him, even if implicitly, and he appreciated it.

Appreciated it and told me he did.

Oh, my heart.

Miles cleared his throat. "You can stop with the swoony eyes. Please. Please stop."

I stood up and ruffled his hair, treating him like the kid he was. "Out. And thank you for the cupcakes."

"Uh-huh. Since you're using them as an excuse for a booty call, you're very welcome." He waggled his eyebrows suggestively.

I shoved him out my front door and closed it firmly in his impertinent face.

10

I settled into Luke's couch.

"Miles accused me of making a booty call."

Luke almost snorted beer out of his nose. As it was, he suffered through a brief coughing fit.

When I'd arrived, I found Luke drinking a beer, so he'd opted to save the cupcakes for later. I'd set aside one for tomorrow and brought Luke three.

"Sorry."

He set his beer bottle down. "This town. Who knows what kind of rumors will be flying tomorrow?"

"Oh, none. Miles won't be spreading gossip, because he won't be mentioning his visit."

Picking his beer bottle up again, Luke said, "I suppose he has some pertinent information, and you convinced him to tell me all."

"About that..." I couldn't ask him to ignore illegal activity, but maybe to prioritize. "You're busy with a murder investigation."

He waited to see where I was going before he agreed, though clearly he *was* busy with a murder investigation. He'd been reviewing witness statements when I'd arrived.

"I'm just thinking, as busy as you're going to be that you won't have a lot of time to be concerned about minor crimes."

"What's he done?"

I'd removed my shoes at the door, and now I tucked my feet up under me. "If I tell you that, and then you arrest the kid for this silly, childish thing he's done, he's not going to want to talk to you about Catie. And if you wait until after, well, I'd feel terrible, because I encouraged him to go to you and spill his guts."

"Is this about the painting on Broad Street?"

Broad Street? The Carson building was over on — "Wait, you know he's been, uh..."

"Defacing abandoned buildings with Matthew Simms?"

"Well, I only knew about the one just outside of town, the old Carson warehouse."

"Oh, yeah. That one's particularly good." He smiled at my surprised reaction. "What? I can't appreciate art?"

"Art...graffiti. Vandalism, really."

"It is, and every once in a while, Bubba pulls Matthew in and has a talk with him, because he used the wrong bit of concrete or brick for a canvas. But when Miles and Matthew work together, they only ever target abandoned or derelict properties, and they do good work. Better than Matthew alone."

"Fair enough. Miles basically said he's mentoring Matthew, though he didn't use that word." I'd been doubtful, because he'd been talking about illegal activity, but it sounded like maybe he had been a positive influence on Matthew's art and his delinquent ways.

"What exactly does Miles's urban art have to do with Catie?"

I couldn't help a smile. "Miles's urban art?"

He rolled his eyes. "Look, at some point they're going to piss someone off enough to be fined, but so far they're more about beautification than destruction, so Bubba doesn't make too much of a fuss."

"But enough to keep them on their toes."

"Basically."

Small-town policing at work, I supposed. "He was worried that his small-time guilt would make him look big-time guilty."

Luke's expression turned thoughtful. "That's actually pretty perceptive. One of the difficulties with this job is that everyone is hiding something, and it's my job to figure out if the secret they're protecting is relevant."

"Sounds exhausting."

"Most days it's not. But when murder is involved...well, yes."

"So you'll go easy on Miles tomorrow?"

He didn't reply, just flashed me an enigmatic smile. The SGG ladies thought I had this great "in" with law enforcement. If only they knew just how little Luke shared, they'd rethink that conclusion.

But thinking of the ladies reminded me of Helen's more fanciful theory, which I couldn't resist sharing with Luke.

"Helen thinks Catie was in witness protection. I think I talked her down, but—" The look on Luke's face stopped me midsentence. "No. She was not."

"No. Of course not." Then he paused. "Actually, if someone in Sage County was in witness protection, I'm not sure I'd know unless there was a problem. Even then, probably not."

"So Catie wasn't in witness protection. Oh. Oh my gosh, I knew it." Well, I hadn't exactly known it, but I'd pitched it to Helen as a viable theory. "She changed her name."

"I didn't say that."

"Hon, you're tired. Your inscrutable cop face isn't as good when you're tired. And you've just confirmed it."

He scrubbed a hand against his jaw. "This doesn't leave the room."

The ladies would hog-tie me and tickle me behind the knees if they found out I'd kept pertinent details to myself.

My indecision must have shown on my face.

"I'm not saying a word unless you guarantee you won't repeat this to the SGG."

I cracked a smile. I couldn't help it. Even Luke called them the SGG. I felt like the little old sleuthing ladies of White Sage, Texas, had won that round.

"Oh, now I'm definitely not telling you." He drained the remainder of his beer. "I'm getting myself a cupcake. You want one?"

"I'm good. I already had one with Miles earlier. But I wouldn't be opposed to a snack." I followed him into the kitchen. "Can I raid your fridge?"

"Of course."

I opened the door and looked inside to find a good number of my favorites. Sure, I remembered to get Luke's favorite beer when I went shopping, but somehow it seemed even more noteworthy that he picked up my brand of fat-free Greek yogurt.

Retrieving a small tub of blueberry, I said, "I promise not to tell Helen and the ladies about whatever secret you've been keeping about Catie's past." I paused, then added, "Though I'm pretty sure it's that she changed her name to escape a shady past."

He stepped behind me, shut the fridge door, and kissed my neck. "She did change her name. After she divorced an extremely wealthy husband in Dallas."

"That explains how the shop, its renovations, and the equipment were all paid for." I turned around inside the circle of his arms.

"Yep. She got a very large settlement." Given my proximity, his expression wasn't at all what I would have expected. It was hard. He stepped back. Then took another step, separating us by a few feet.

My stomach had a funny feeling. "So why change her name? I mean, I changed mine after the divorce, but just back to my maiden name. I didn't hide the fact that I'm from Austin."

I knew one reason she might, and I hoped I was wrong.

"As much of a jerk as your husband was, he didn't put you in the hospital with life-threatening injuries." He grabbed a small plate from the counter with a salted caramel cupcake on it and picked up his water bottle.

It had been a gift from me, the water bottle. Part of my effort to wean him from store-bought water. Now he used refillable bottles and a decent filter pitcher. Not that he'd been difficult to convince.

So much better for the environment and less trash to deal with and...

My distraction technique wasn't working.

Sometimes, if I focused on the little details right in front of me, I could separate myself from a larger ugliness that loomed.

But my stomach wasn't having it. Poor Catie. Bubbly, sweet Catie had been hurt by the person who was supposed to love her best, and it made me sick. Angry. Frustrated.

Had her ex come back to finish the job?

Once we'd both settled, me on the couch again and Luke on his favorite well-padded armchair, he said, "She came to both Bubba and me when she moved here. She wanted us to be familiar with her background, in case there was any kind of trouble. I haven't told anyone else, and to the best of my knowledge, neither has he."

"I'm betting that's why she had a will. Being seriously injured can make a person more aware of such things."

"You know about the will?"

"Steph mentioned it earlier today when I was in the shop. She said the fate of the shop would be determined by the will, but that they hadn't been able to get in touch with Catie's attorney."

"Angela inherits." Luke misinterpreted my surprise and explained, "She wasn't close to her family. They didn't support her through the divorce. Thought she should stick it out."

"What? After her husband put her in the hospital?"

"Yeah, like I said, she wasn't close with them. Cut ties entirely when she moved here. She'd been living in Louisiana for a while, but they were trying to get her to reconcile, so she changed her name and moved here after the divorce was final. Anyway, Angela must have seemed like a good idea in the absence of any family to inherit."

"Yeah. I can see that. How do you know Angela inherits?"

"She told me."

I nodded. "That's what Miles is coming to talk to you about tomorrow. It's interesting that Steph doesn't know the contents of the will, and Miles only knows by accident. Any reason Angela hasn't set their minds at ease?" One reason came to mind. "She's not thinking of shutting it down and selling, is she?"

"I don't think so. I think it's more to do with having legal confirmation. She didn't want to make any assertions until it was official."

I nodded. "So she's a suspect, right? Because she has motive. And Catie's ex..."

"We're working on finding out where he was at the time of the murder." Luke leaned forward. "Do not poke around in Catie's past. Don't try to find out who her husband was. Don't look for any connections to her past. You don't want to meet this man."

"Men who beat their wives are bullies, Luke. I don't have anything to fear from someone like that. It's all about power and control, something he wouldn't have outside of his marriage."

"You didn't read the arrest report." His eyes clouded. "You didn't see the pictures."

Which made no sense. If there were official records of what he'd done... "If she reported it, how is this guy not in jail?"

"She decided not to testify. The ADA almost pursued it without her, planning to rely on the medical records alone, but that's not a good idea. It's a good way to lose a case, especially against someone with exceptional legal counsel."

"I don't understand. I mean, I do understand not reporting it. But to have the courage to go to the police and then not follow through... I'm not sure I get that."

"She leveraged the threat of criminal prosecution to get a very fast, very lucrative divorce. She told me she had no regrets about how she handled it. And I'm not about to judge her for making the right decision for herself."

"Even if that means he does it again."

He smiled grimly. "Her family wasn't supportive.

His, oddly enough, was. And his family has a lot of money. I think she might have created some difficulties for him with his family. I suspect they'll keep a close eye on him in the future. And he's supposedly going to counseling."

It was mind-boggling to discover all of this had been simmering under the cheerful surface of the woman so few of us had actually known. "She told you all of this when she moved here?"

"No. She gave Bubba and me the basics, and we both chatted with her regularly. I know Bubba called her every week. And when she dropped the cupcakes by every other week, we talked."

My heart went all pitter-patter. "You were worried about her, here in a new town, all by herself, with no support."

"Of course. So was Bubba. And she didn't have anyone to talk to about her past." He shrugged.

"Right, because she didn't want her real identity dropped into the stream of gossip that runs rampant here. Smart lady."

He rubbed the back of his neck. "Yeah."

He looked so tired. So sad.

"You know this isn't your fault?"

He looked up, surprised. "I know that. The person at fault is the person who killed her. There's no question of that in my mind. But I liked her. I respected her. I'm just so…"

"Mad? Sad? Exhausted by the violence?"

"Yeah. All of that." He got up from his armchair and sat next to me on the sofa, where he held me for several minutes.

Sometimes you just needed to hold someone or be held by someone.

When I left, sleepy and warm, to get into my car and make the short drive home, I had a new number one suspect.

I didn't know his name or what he looked like, but I knew he'd hurt Catie before and badly.

Now I just had to figure out the details. Alone.

I couldn't let Helen, Vanessa, or Georgie anywhere near this guy.

11

Zella leaves me at home sometimes.

Too often.

I should go with her all the time.

Car rides are fun, and she's lonely without me, and car rides are fun.

I'm the best dog of all the dogs. She tells me so all the time.

But this time, when she comes back, she smells like Luke.

A car ride without me?

A visit to Luke without me?

Maybe I wasn't the best dog of all the dogs.

12

When I got home from Luke's, Fairmont wasn't his usual happily mellow self.

He almost seemed mopey.

He followed me around the house as I prepared for bed, but his gait and gaze weren't as animated as usual. Even his tail carriage was off. His tail was...droopy.

"I'm sorry I didn't bring you with me." I grabbed my laptop and e-reader and headed to the bedroom.

I'd been treating him differently all day long. I hadn't realized it, but in retrospect, it was clear to see. And I knew why.

I was terrified that there was someone, some family, out there missing him.

I was scared they'd want him back.

And I was already sad about losing him, even though he was still here.

Ridiculous, but there it was.

I crawled into bed and, for once, flipped the duvet over so that Fairmont could crawl into bed with me.

He looked at the spot I'd made for him under the covers, then at me, then at the spot.

I'd fussed at him for burrowing under my duvet countless times at the old house and then again when we'd moved, and he'd "forgotten" that wasn't allowed. "New context, new rules" was how his doggie brain seemed to view it.

I patted the spot next to me, and that chased away any reservations. He was on my bed and curled into a spotted ball of fur next to me faster than I could say, "Who's the best dog ever?"

Once I'd pulled the duvet cover over both of us and propped myself up on my pillows, I opened up my laptop and checked my inbox.

There were two responses to my inquiry email, both stating they had no team members who'd lost a search dog recently and suggesting I check for a microchip if I was looking for a previous owner.

The shelter had chipped Fairmont, because they hadn't found one when he'd come in as a stray. Of course they'd checked. Of course I'd asked. But I appreciated that the people who'd answered were trying to help. I replied to both, thanking them for their time and recommendations.

Then I set my laptop aside and picked up my e-reader, loaded with Vanessa and Georgie's latest mystery, book nine in their most popular series. I thought for sure they'd incorporate their recent personal experiences in their latest work, and they had, but only very small pieces. They hadn't done anything so overt as writing about a neighbor found in the backyard or a philandering poet found in his temporary digs.

Their murder mystery was much more fanciful and all the more fun for not reminding of the real-life murders of White Sage. I'd had a front-row seat to those deaths and didn't want to relive them in my late-night reading.

Fairmont curled his soft, warm body closer, and I read my worries away until my eyes grew heavy.

I woke to a loud banging on my front door. I wouldn't call it knocking, more like a fist pounding against the solid wood.

Apparently, Fairmont had been in as deep a sleep as I had, because I was blinking myself awake, just about to tell whoever was making such a fuss to stop, when Fairmont finally hopped off my bed barking.

"A little late, buddy." My voice sounded thick and

sleepy. I cleared my throat and hollered, "I'm coming."

Only after the words had escaped did I realize that such aggression in the middle of the night might be indicative of a less-than-friendly visitor.

My fears were immediately laid to rest when Geraldine yelled, "Hurry up! We have an emergency."

Since an emergency in Geraldine's world could very easily include Luke—Luke injured, Luke in trouble...worse I wouldn't even contemplate—I ran to the front door, stomping on Fairmont's unfinished cheese chew on the way.

I answered the door in my PJs, clutching my injured foot, likely looking as if the sky was falling.

Geraldine took one look at me and said, "Luke's fine."

And I let out a breath I didn't know I'd been holding.

"Well, not exactly fine. You need to get dressed and come with me. I need reinforcements. I never know exactly what's going on between the two of you, but you're a much better choice than Helen."

I'd been woken from a deep sleep, my foot was throbbing, and even Fairmont was discombobulated. He was pacing anxiously between Geraldine and me, nosing our hands.

Given my state, it was no wonder I was having a

hard time catching up with Geraldine. "Why do you need reinforcements? And what time is it?"

"Maybe midnight or one? I'm not sure. I've been calling you for the last twenty minutes, but I guess your phone is dead. It kept rolling to voicemail."

Probably because I forgot to plug it in before I went to bed.

Geraldine stared hard at my tank top, then my bare toes. "You need to get dressed. Right now." She made shooing motions with her hands.

"Not until you tell me what you need reinforcements for, and where we're going."

"We're going to the county lockup, which is where Luke and Bubba are."

"What's happened? Why is Bubba even up at this hour?" Bubba wasn't in charge of the case, though I was sure he was helping Luke.

"Because Luke's gone and arrested him." When my jaw dropped, she added, "For assault."

I covered my face with my hands, because I was in no state of mind to consider the implications of that statement.

Actually, yes, I was. That was bad.

Bubba was loved by everyone but Helen and Geraldine, and those two had their reasons. Reasons that had nothing to do with Bubba Charleston, chief of White Sage Police Department, and everything to do with choices and decisions made a very, very long time ago by a young man who was a very different person from the chief I knew.

Luke was equally liked and respected. And as far as I knew, the two men got along really well. If it turned out that Luke really was Bubba's son, I wouldn't be shocked. They shared several character-istics. More than just their height and good looks. They were both kind, smart, generous men.

Men who took their jobs very seriously.

"Bubba wouldn't do that. He's...he's..."

"Not usually such a complete and utter idiot. Yes. Well, he's gone and punched a tourist, so Luke arrested his ornery ass."

Oh my. That was...unexpected.

It was Friday night, and White Sage did pull in a good weekend crowd. There was a fishing tourna-ment this weekend, as well, and the weekenders could be a handful, but Bubba was the last person I'd expect to get physical with a rowdy tourist.

"Why are we going to the county lockup?" Because we were going. If Geraldine thought we needed to be there, we needed to be there. I was filling my electric kettle with water for a pot of coffee as I asked.

"Luke's taken Bubba there instead of the jail, thank goodness. And someone needs to talk sense to Bubba. Clearly that person isn't the man who just arrested him." She pulled a travel mug from my cupboard. "Go get dressed."

Fairmont wavered for a moment—coffee in the morning meant breakfast was soon to follow, and breakfast happened in the kitchen—but he must have realized that the timing was all wrong. That, or he could tell that I was upset, because he followed me into the bathroom and then my room while I got ready.

"I don't know what's going on, buddy, but nothing good. I can tell you that."

When I returned to the kitchen, I gave Fairmont a handful of kibble to eat while I sipped from the travel mug of coffee Geraldine had prepared for me. It had just the right amount of hemp milk to cut the bitterness of the coffee.

"You ready?"

"Yes. Can Fairmont come? We can take my car, and he'll be fine in the back."

"Oh, yes. I parked in the street. I just assumed."

As I attached Fairmont's leash, I realized that I hadn't asked about the tourist who'd managed to push Bubba's buttons. Bubba had plenty of experience dealing with belligerent drunks and aggressive jerks. It had to take a special sort of person to make him lose his professional cool.

"I don't suppose you know who this guy is that Bubba punched?"

Geraldine sighed. "Not really. Just some wealthy businessman down from Dallas. Dave Zapata said his car cost more than most houses around this area."

So Dave had been Geraldine's source. That boy was going to be in so much trouble with Luke. If he wasn't blabbing to his own mama, he was apparently giving Luke's mom the scoop.

Wait... "Dallas? You're sure?"

"Yeah. That's what Dave said. Why?"

A wealthy Dallas businessman, here just after Catie's murder (perhaps arriving before Catie's murder?), who happened to push the normally even-tempered Bubba Charleston to violence.

I squeezed my eyes shut. Had Bubba just brawled with Catie's abusive ex? Possibly her killer?

Geraldine poked me hard in the ribs.

"Ow." I rubbed the spot gently. That might leave a bruise.

"What do you know?"

Nothing I could share, because I'd promised Luke. I'd promised I wouldn't say a word.

But maybe Bubba would.

13

"Why can't we see him?" Geraldine demanded.

Luke took an audible breath. "Because he's cooling off in a cell, and he doesn't need the two of you riling him up."

If he'd looked tired earlier this evening, or rather yesterday evening, since it was now in the wee hours of Saturday morning, he looked exhausted now.

I walked around his desk and kissed him on the cheek, since neither Geraldine nor I had offered him a proper greeting when we'd walked into his office.

He closed his eyes, just for a moment, but when he opened them, he looked more relaxed.

I unsnapped Fairmont's leash from his collar as Geraldine relinquished the travel mug of coffee she'd made for Luke at my house. She'd been holding it hostage.

"You know, we don't actually allow dogs." But then he rubbed Fairmont behind the ears.

Fairmont rested his chin on Luke's thigh and stared adoringly at him.

"Humph." Geraldine crossed her arms. "He's basically deputized at this point."

"I was going to leave him in the car, but Geraldine—"

"Thought that was ridiculous." She rolled her eyes. What she'd actually said was: "Luke could probably use some cheering up."

"He loves coming here. All the deputies adore him. I think he gets more attention here than just about anywhere else." And that was saying a lot, because wherever we went, people stopped to comment on how handsome he was and to pet him. He was friendly, polite, and something of a celebrity in White Sage.

He'd gotten excited when we were still a few streets away from Luke's office. I swore he knew where we'd been headed, even though he'd only been two or three times before. He'd shoved his nose into the crack of the passenger window and wagged his tail furiously right up until I'd let him out of the SUV.

"If you're not going to let us see Bubba," Geraldine said, "then you can at least tell me why some fancy-pants businessman from Dallas set him off. She won't tell me." Geraldine gave me a pointed look of disapproval.

I was immune. Growing up with my parents, who'd disapproved of anything less than perfection, it was either develop a thick skin or wallow in low self-worth.

"How did you find out about Bubba's altercation?" Luke drilled his mom with a probing look.

"Not saying. I protect my sources."

"Dave and I are going to have a serious chat." He gave Fairmont a last pet and then focused all of his attention on his mother. "Do you want to tell me why you think the chief would have any interest in talking to you?"

Geraldine's lips thinned.

Excellent question. It's not like she and the chief were on good terms. I'd have asked the question myself if she hadn't ambushed me in the middle of the night. I wasn't at my best when woken from a deep sleep.

"We're much friendlier these days," Geraldine said.

Luke arched an eyebrow. "I've never understood your issue with him. He's a good guy. A good chief of police."

"When he's not punching tourists," Geraldine muttered.

Luke looked pissed—and not at his mom. "Let's just say he might have been provoked."

He wouldn't make eye contact with me, and that was when I knew: Bubba's altercation had absolutely been with Catie's ex, and it had absolutely been about Catie.

I took a breath and let it out slowly. Then another and another. When I thought my voice might come out sounding somewhat natural, I said, "I don't suppose you know when that tourist arrived in town?"

Luke blinked, then looked at me with his cop expression firmly in place. "I'm working on verifying that particular piece of information."

"You know your mom isn't really one to overreact, so if she thinks it's a good idea to visit Bubba, maybe you should let us poke our heads in and say hi?"

Dave was Geraldine's source, and he was solid. Young, talked too much, told his mother everything, but his information was spot-on. And whatever he'd told Geraldine had her pounding on my door in the middle of the night demanding I accompany her to "talk some sense into him."

"Please." I didn't directly interfere with Luke's job. Indirectly, yes, and only with great encouragement from the SGG. I didn't pressure him to tell me things he oughtn't. So me asking for this was unusual.

"Five minutes. I'll keep Fairmont here. A deputy will show you the way. I'm pretty sure Bubba doesn't want to see me right now."

A young deputy, one I recognized but didn't know by name, appeared only a minute or so after Luke called him.

He escorted us without any chitchat at all. He looked about as serious as a twenty-something in a deputy's uniform could look. If I had to guess, he wasn't particularly happy about having the chief of White Sage's small police force in county lockup.

There were only a few cells on site. The deputies called it lockup to differentiate it from Sage County's jail, which was a little outside of town.

Lockup was really just an extension of the sheriff's office, so we didn't have far to go. The deputy pointed to the end of a row of four cells. "He's the only one we've got in tonight, and I'm not about to move him to an interrogation room right now."

What did that mean?

But he was gone before either of us could ask.

I followed Geraldine to the chief's cell and heard her mutter, "Oh, John. What were you thinking?"

John? Since when was Bubba Charleston *John*?

"Dina, what are you doing here?" Bubba Charleston did not look like himself.

For the second time since I'd known him, the chief had a black eye. Geraldine had given him the last one, but there was truly no comparison.

This black eye wasn't a little discoloration from a facial bruise that happened to settle around his eye. His eye was swollen from a solid hit. His hair and clothes were also rumpled. He looked disreputable —but not drunk. He didn't stand as we approached. He remained seated on a surprisingly clean-looking cot-type bed.

"I'm here because you've gone and got yourself arrested. Dave said Luke had a hell of a time getting the cuffs on you, too."

The chief touched his eye.

"Oh, John. Please tell me Luke didn't hit you."

"Luke *didn't* hit me. Dave Zapata did."

A small "eep" of surprise tumbled from my lips. I covered my mouth, but too late. Dave Zapata was the last person I'd expect to throw a punch. And didn't law enforcement officers get training on how to subdue their quarry? Surely that didn't involve punching them.

"Zella." The chief tipped his head in my direction.

"I'm sorry for your troubles, chief."

"Humph. We'll see how long that title sticks after

tonight." He leaned his elbows on his knees and clasped his hands. Without looking at either of us, he said, "Maybe it's time for me to retire anyway."

"No."

Geraldine's firm denial surprised both the chief and me.

That piqued Bubba's interest. He looked at Geraldine, and for the first time since we'd arrived, his expression lightened. "You don't think I'm getting too old for the job?"

I was almost certain Geraldine was going to make a crack about how incompetent he was. That was her normal schtick every time Bubba's name came up. "John Charleston, you are good for this town, and you know it. You can't retire."

Both the chief and I had the same reaction: shock.

"Stop it." Geraldine frowned. "You know you're good at your job."

"Oh, I know I am." He looked around the cell then added with a wry twist to his lips, "Usually. But you're the last person I'd expect to acknowledge it."

She rolled her eyes. Then, much more seriously, she said, "Why? Why would you do something that would risk your job? You have more sense than that."

And the compliments just kept coming. Geraldine really didn't like seeing the chief locked up. If Helen was right about the history between these two, then it wasn't completely surprising that Geraldine's feelings would be complicated.

"Hang on a sec." I followed a hypothetical in my head for a moment. "Is your job at risk if the person you assaulted is in no position to testify? If the person is charged with, for example, a murder?"

Geraldine's head whipped around. "What do you know?"

I took a breath, turned calmly to face her—then did my best to lie without lying. "I don't *know* anything. I'm posing a question. That's all."

Bubba heaved a sigh. "Luke's looking into his movements over the past few days." He looked at me. "But the chances of me being formally charged are slim if Heath Carson is charged with—or better yet, convicted of—murder."

Bubba Charleston, chief of the White Sage Police Department, had just asked for my help. He'd been arrested, but not charged. And maybe, hopefully, we could make sure he wouldn't be.

That man was no one's fool. He knew name-dropping Catie's abusive ex—and there was no longer any doubt in my mind that Heath Carson was Catie's ex—would set Geraldine, me, and the SGG on Carson's trail.

Did the chief not trust that Luke would do his job? That didn't seem right.

The question must have been written all over my

face, because the chief said, "Luke will handle everything exactly as he should: legally. Which can be
slow."

Geraldine touched my arm. "They can only hold
him for twenty-four hours, then they'll let him go or
charge him. But that's not the real issue. Other than
an actual conviction, the real issue is gossip and
public opinion. If this can get cleared up quickly,
basically making it clear that charges won't be
brought, then John's reputation will take less of a
hit."

"But chief of police isn't an elected position,
right?" I knew that Luke's position as sheriff *was*
elected, and that this type of scenario would be like
crack for any opponent he'd face in the future.

"No, but if there's enough of a fuss, the city
manager would have to fire him. Even if John can
legally keep his job, the city manager won't keep him
if there's not public support."

Everyone *loved* the chief. Except Geraldine was
right: White Sage loved gossip, and it was quite
possible the town loved a good tale more than they
adored their chief of police. In which case...

"Got it," I said. "If this Heath Carson person
murdered Catie, we'll find out."

"Just a little look around. No more. And Zella,
Dina? Carson is not someone any of you ladies need

to be around alone." Bubba gave me a hard look. "You understand?"

"Yes." I hadn't seen Catie's medical records, but I'd seen the look on Luke's face when he talked about them. "I understand."

We didn't have a chance to talk about anything else, because the same young deputy returned and hustled Geraldine and me out of lockup and into Luke's office.

Fairmont removed himself from Luke's lap when he saw us.

He was such a good dog. He only ever jumped up when invited, so Luke must have needed some dog cuddles.

"Please tell me that you'll both go home and get some sleep now." Luke attached Fairmont's leash as he waited for us to respond.

That was an easy promise to make. "I'm exhausted. I'm definitely going straight to bed." I took Fairmont's leash from him and leaned down to pet him.

He sat next to me and leaned his head against my knee. Even Fairmont was tired.

"Mom?" Luke prompted, when she didn't immediately chime in.

"Oh, yes. I need to get a few hours before I have to serve breakfast. I've got a handful of hikers and several fishermen staying at The Hiker this weekend."

Ever since her cook had died, Geraldine had paired up with her one permanent boarder, Hank, to provide all of the meals for her guests. Hank had revealed a surprising skill for cooking, and Geraldine handled serving and cleanup. The two made a pretty good meal service pair.

Geraldine pulled Luke in for a tight hug. As she stepped away, she said, "I forgive you for arresting Bubba. I'm sure you didn't have any other choice."

He cocked his head, looking at his mother with some confusion. Which when I realized that if what Helen had said was true, if Bubba Charleston was truly Luke's biological father, Luke didn't seem to have a clue.

I had to wonder how much he knew about his mother and Bubba's history. If he was even aware they'd dated.

His gaze met mine. He had questions. Questions he wasn't going to raise in front of his mother.

I shrugged, then leaned in to kiss him. This time I skipped his cheek. My guy deserved a proper kiss. "I'll talk to you tomorrow."

"Sounds good. Oh, I'll need some help with Turbo, the chief's pup, tomorrow. He asked if I could keep an eye on him while he's otherwise occupied. Think you might be able to help?" When he saw the look on my face, he cracked a grin. "Don't worry. I've got the morning covered."

Thank goodness. I wasn't a morning person in the best of circumstances, and these were so very far removed from the best.

Geraldine made it all the way to the car. She even managed to wait until I'd loaded Fairmont in the back, climbed into the driver's seat, and clicked my seatbelt in place.

But as soon as I put the SUV into drive, she said, "Spill. Right now, Griselda Marek. Right this instant."

"How do you even know my full name?" Probably Helen. Helen knew my full name before I'd even moved in. The advantage of having a daughter who was a real estate agent in a small town.

"No deflections. Who is this Heath Carson? Why did Bubba hit him? And why are you being so cagey?"

"Bubba? I thought he was John," I said, never taking my eyes from the road.

"Don't you even start. I want answers."

"Which I can't give you."

"Can't or won't?"

I considered that. I'd made a promise. I truly couldn't tell her, not without violating that promise. "Can't."

"It's to do with Luke's work, isn't it? He's told you something in confidence."

I didn't reply. Couldn't really, because any answer would be confirmation or a lie.

She grumbled, then dug her phone out of the depths of her purse.

Which reminded me that I needed to charge mine when I got home. I hadn't bothered to bring it with me since it was dead, and Geraldine had hers.

"How many Heath Carsons from Dallas can there be?" she muttered as she poked at her phone.

Excellent question. One I hoped she quickly discovered. I also hoped she happened to find some intel on *our* Heath Carson. Because I'd love to know more about the piece of human refuse who'd put his own wife in the hospital and quite possibly killed her.

As she continued to jab at her phone, she said, "Bubba doesn't have a temper. Not at all. And he's not violent. I didn't even know he knew how to punch someone."

That seemed extreme. The man had to be sixty-three or sixty-four. It would be unusual if, in the course of those sixty-some-odd years, he hadn't had cause or inclination to strike another person.

And he was a police officer. He had to have training in restraint and self-defense, and that had to include some offensive measures. Probably. I'd have to remember to ask Luke about that at some point.

As for the chief having no temper... Everyone got angry, even people not known to have a temper. And when faced with the man who'd done terrible things to his own wife, a woman the chief had come to know and like, a woman that man might have brutally murdered... Yeah, I could see even-tempered Bubba Charleston losing it and decking that man.

"You are a terrible friend." Geraldine's words contained no heat, so I took them for the expression of frustration that they were.

"Um-hm. Terrible. I'll remember that the next time you come knocking on my door in the middle of the night." I glanced at her. "And shame on you for using me to get in to see the chief. You knew Luke wouldn't let you see him on your own."

"True." She sounded distracted. Either she'd found Carson, or she was on his trail. A few seconds later she hollered, "Yes!" but then fell completely silent.

"What? What did you find?"

"I found Heath Carson, prominent Dallas businessman, and husband of Marie Kathleen Carson." There was no inflection in her tone. No dismay over seeing Catie using a different name.

She quietly scrolled for the remainder of the drive to my house.

Once I'd parked, I said, "Well?"

"Marie Kathleen either has a twin sister or Catie changed her name at some point in the last two years."

Again, I couldn't deny or confirm knowledge, so I said nothing.

"There are a lot of pictures. The Carsons were very active in the Dallas social scene." Still her tone revealed nothing.

"And?"

She looked at me. "And Catie looks sad in all of them."

I just bet she did.

"She's smiling, but she's sad. Anyone who knew Catie, our Catie, would see it." Geraldine smiled slightly. "And her hair is blonde."

I returned her smile and squeezed her forearm. "Well, then, that's not our Catie. Our Catie thought blonde was boring."

Geraldine left after extracting a promise that I'd check in with her in the morning, after her hikers and fishermen were fed and off to their various adventures.

And I went to bed, because I was thoroughly and completely done with this day.

One thing I did do, however, before going to bed: I emailed the SGG Heath Carson's name. His name and the most basic of facts concerning the chief's arrest.

With Geraldine in possession of that information, it would most certainly make its way to the SGG. And this way, they'd receive as unbiased an account as possible.

But also, Helen, Vanessa, and Georgie could be quite early risers. And with Vanessa and Georgie on a writing deadline, their help would be limited to research in between writing sprints.

With any luck, I'd wake up to some new information about Heath Carson.

14

I watch my lady sleep.

She likes to sleep even more than I do. Usually, she sleeps quietly.

She curls on her side.

She lies on her back.

Sometimes she hugs a pillow, sometimes me.

But this morning she snuffles and rolls around like an unsettled puppy.

Her friends, my friends, are visiting. I hear the familiar rumble of their cars, and as they near the house I can smell them through a crack in the window. They smell like sugar and butter and flour and love.

Should I wake her?

She likes visits from her friends, but she likes sleeping, too.

I watch her as the knocking begins.

She pulls a pillow over her head and pretends she can't hear it, but it's very loud.

15

My head thudded uncomfortably.

Waking with a headache was the worst. Especially when one hadn't earned that headache by consuming excessive amounts of whisky or tequila.

I hadn't consumed excessive amounts of whisky or tequila...had I?

Then I realized the banging wasn't inside my head, but rather on my front door.

That was a relief, minus the fact that once again someone felt the need to wake me from a deep sleep by playing the drums on my door.

I lifted the pillow from my head, probably placed there subconsciously when the knocking began, and yelled, "Just a minute."

As I hunted the covers for my phone, I realized

I'd plugged it in to charge when I'd gotten home last night...and likely not turned it on.

I also realized that Fairmont was curled up at my feet, completely unconcerned by the commotion at the door. I eyed him quizzically, but he simple gazed back without lifting his head, watching, waiting.

We were definitely playing the "who's getting up first" game.

"You take your time, dear," Georgie called.

Which explained Fairmont's behavior. Georgie didn't fall into the category of persons deserving of an alarm bark. And he must have already been awake when she—or whoever was with her—had knocked on the door. Otherwise, he'd have fussed when startled awake.

"But not too long. You should get us a spare key —or the key code." That nugget of nonsense came from Helen.

I certainly wouldn't get them a key or give them my code. They'd have shown up even earlier if they had unfettered access. I'd bet my morning coffee on it.

I scrubbed my hands across my face, avoiding the tender and slightly puffy skin around my eyes.

Fairmont huffed out a sympathetic sigh.

Helen, Georgie, and most likely Vanessa were gathered on my small front porch waiting for an update, and I was in no state of mind to keep Luke's secrets or be discreet.

Then I remembered the email.

My late-night self was a foolish, foolish woman.

Instead of waking to the email I'd expected, I was getting the whole gang in person. And if I'd been thinking clearly last night, I'd have realized that was a likely possibility.

Helen couldn't resist being right in the midst of any investigation. And Georgie and Vanessa's deadline was either not as pressing as they'd implied, or those ladies had typed their fingers raw yesterday in order to get ahead.

I swung my feet to the floor, and the standoff was over. Fairmont was off the bed and headed for the front door like a shot.

I debated making them wait on the porch while I sorted myself out a bit, then decided we were good enough friends that they could see my unfiltered morning self.

"Oh my," Georgie said, taking in my appearance from head to toe and back up again. She clutched a covered dish to her chest in dismay.

Vanessa entered without her cane, a notable improvement, since she'd almost certainly walked from Georgie's, several houses away. "Your watchdog doesn't do much watchdogging, does he?"

But then she stopped to pet Fairmont, so he

knew she still loved him whatever his failings in home security.

"Nonsense," Helen said. She also held a peace offering: a Tupperware container with some tasty treat, I was sure. "Fairmont is an exceptional watch-dog. He must have known it was us."

"Yes," I agreed, "I'm sure he did, but he doesn't always bark at visitors at the door."

Helen gave me a look much like the one Georgie had, full of dismay after taking in my appearance, and headed straight for the kitchen. "Coffee," she called as she marched forward with her Tupperware in hand. "You definitely need coffee."

Georgie hurried after Helen, still clutching the covered dish to her chest. "I'll do that. Your coffee is good, but..."

Helen's laugh was all I heard as the two took over my kitchen.

Vanessa and Fairmont stayed in the living room with me.

"Don't you have a book to write?" I squatted down to Fairmont's level and hugged his neck.

She gave me a critical look. "Don't you have a shower to take?"

I ran a hand through my hair to find it sticking up on one side and flat on the other. "Well, it is... What time is it?"

"A little after nine. You sent that email in the

middle of the night, so Georgie convinced Helen and me to let you sleep in."

"Until nine," I replied with a hint of wryness.

"Helen and I wanted to come by at seven. You can thank Georgie for those two extra hours, especially since it gave me time to bake cinnamon rolls." She had a pinched look. "I don't think you're going to like what we found. Or rather, what we suspect."

I didn't say anything. Couldn't say anything. My hope was that they'd reach their own conclusions about Catie and her past, a conclusion that approached the truth, so that we could move forward together in our unofficial investigation.

Vanessa's eyes narrowed. "You know. Humph. That's email for you; hides more than it says. Give me a face-to-face conversation every time."

I continued to pet Fairmont, who seemed to be enjoying the attention even though he hadn't had his morning bathroom break or his breakfast. I murmured, "Good dog," next to his ear.

His tail went into overdrive.

Someone hadn't gotten nearly enough attention and affection yesterday, and I'd make sure to rectify that oversight today. Whatever the future held for us, he was mine for now and he deserved all the love.

His wet nose nudged my ear.

I chuckled at the tickling sensation. "Breakfast?"

And just like that, he was off to the kitchen.

Vanessa chuckled. "That dog has his priorities sorted just the way they ought to be. You go take a shower. I'll let him out in the yard for a minute."

"I need to feed him." I'd just promised him food, and in the world of dogs, that was a serious promise indeed.

"No problem. I know where you keep the dog food."

I eyed her suspiciously. "One level scoop. Food is not love." Which wasn't exactly true, especially given the treats I'd spotted in Georgie and Helen's hands, so I said, "Excessive food is not love."

Vanessa shook her head. "Baked goods are definitely love."

"Well, yes, but you know what I mean." I wasn't about to argue and risk losing a chance at those cinnamon rolls. Also, Vanessa's baked goods *were* love. It was one of the many ways she expressed her affection for her favorite people. She might be more taciturn than Georgie, but her heart was just as big.

When I'd finished an abbreviated morning routine, I found coffee waiting, as well as reheated cinnamon rolls and some garlic cheddar biscuits that Helen said were a snap to make.

Easy to make or not, they were delicious.

We sat down and enjoyed the food as Fairmont watched from his dog bed. By unspoken agreement, none of us broached the unpleasant topic of Heath Carson until we'd all finished eating.

But the moment I'd swallowed my last bite, Helen said, "Tell her. I think she already knows, but tell her."

Vanessa gave her empty plate a last longing look —she'd only allowed herself half a cinnamon roll— then said, "Fine. When we looked Heath Carson up on the Google, we found pictures. Pictures of him and Catie, except she went by a different name. And Heath Carson was charged—"

"But not convicted," Georgie interjected.

"Right. Charged, but not convicted, of assault with family violence."

"Vanessa." The suspicion in my voice must have warned her, because she wouldn't quite meet my gaze. "Didn't you just tell me the other day that background checks available to the public only show convictions?"

"I might have said that, yes," she agreed, still without looking at me directly.

Georgie leaned forward and whispered, "We have a source."

Vanessa rolled her eyes and, at a completely normal volume level, said, "Yes. We do. And it's not illegal or anything. Just a little iffy."

Not illegal. Just a little iffy.

Why was I surprised? They wrote mysteries to

pad their meager Social Security checks. Not romance, not women's fiction, not cute stories with cats—mysteries. They were also part of a social group called the Sleuthing Granny Gang. Naturally, they had iffy background-check sources.

It was too early for this. Or rather, I hadn't had enough caffeine.

"Refill?" Helen asked with an amused glint in her eyes.

"Please." There was a tinge of desperation in my voice; I never claimed to be a morning person. "Whatever your sources say, we know for a fact that Chief Charleston felt compelled to punch Carson when he encountered him at a local bar last night."

"The same man who was once married to Catie and was charged with domestic violence." Helen's tone made it clear she knew exactly why Bubba had felt compelled to strike such a man.

"So..." Georgie leaned forward on the table. "Tell us how you heard about the chief's arrest. Vanessa and I were already in bed for the night."

"So was I." I added a dollop of hemp milk from the carton on the table after I'd freshened up my coffee. "I don't know how Geraldine found out the chief had been arrested, but she was concerned about"—I stumbled over what was safe to share with the SGG and sipped some coffee to cover my fumble

—"Luke and the chief's working relationship, since Luke had to arrest him."

That sounded reasonable, and it didn't point the finger at any shenanigans between Geraldine and "John" Charleston. Shenanigans of the romantic variety that I was half convinced might be happening in the here and now and not just in the couple's past.

But I wouldn't say a word until Geraldine was ready for her private business to be out in the world. The pressure of the town's expectations hadn't helped my relationship with Luke when we'd started seeing one another, and I was sure it wouldn't help theirs.

"Fair enough, especially if Bubba is Luke's— Ow!" Georgie reached under the table to rub her leg. Then she frowned at Vanessa. "As if Zella doesn't already know. Or at least have her suspicions like the rest of us."

I set my coffee mug down and leaned back in my chair. After sizing up the three ladies at the table, I said, "We can all agree that we have Luke's best interests at heart." I waited for them to agree—with varying degrees of enthusiasm—before proceeding. "None of us knows if Chief Charleston is Luke's father. No one knows the answer to that question except Geraldine and, possibly, the chief."

"But most of the town suspects." Georgie's

comment wasn't mean-spirited. Georgie didn't have it in her. It was simply a statement of fact.

"Rumors aren't always true," I reminded my friendly gang of gossips. "Remember all the nastiness about Penny Richardson? All those rumors, and yet she didn't have a thing to do with the troll war against that author."

Georgie nodded. "That's true, and I still feel bad about that." She brightened. "Vanessa and I had her over for coffee and pie last week."

Vanessa had the sense to look sheepish. "We felt bad that she'd been falsely accused. But she's still power hungry and can be a bully."

"We're learning to stand up to her," Georgie said with a nod.

Vanessa patted her hand. "That's right. And she's a good president, for all that she's forced the vote the last several elections."

The inner workings of small-town writing organizations were much more complicated than I'd ever have guessed.

"So we're agreed?" I asked. "No more speculation about Luke and the chief's relationship to one another." As everyone was set to agree, I added, "Even amongst ourselves."

Helen sighed. "If you think it best." Implying that she didn't think we needed to go quite so far, but she was willing to agree for the sake of friendship. "Now, about this wife-beating scum, Heath Carson. I assume he's our number one suspect."

Georgie heaved a dramatic sigh. "Our only suspect. Though he is a good one. I'm pretty sure he did it." This from the woman who typically believed the best of everyone. Then again, she didn't know Carson personally.

But Carson wasn't our only suspect, and that reminded me that I'd failed to inform the SGG of my conversation with Miles. "Our top suspect, but not our only one."

Once I'd filled them in on my conversation with Miles—omitting his graffiti mentoring admission and listening to their grumblings about letting a man into my home late at night—Georgie said, "But Angela's so sweet. I'm sure she couldn't have had anything to do with it."

Helen and Vanessa shared a glance.

"You don't agree?" I hadn't mentioned Miles's "White Sage losers" comment. It was an unkind sentiment that lacked any real basis. Unless there *was* some basis...?

Vanessa deferred to Helen, but Helen didn't immediately leap in with an accusation. She gave her words a good deal of consideration before she spoke. "Angela is a hard worker, and we've seen that at Catie's Cupcakery. At least some of the success of the shop is on her shoulders."

I waited. Helen didn't typically need much encouragement to dish, so either my request to keep mum about Luke and the chief's speculated biological connection had dampened her enthusiasm for gossip (doubtful), or she felt conflicted about Angela.

Finally, with a small grimace, she said, "But Angela isn't a people person. She doesn't get along well with others."

"I don't know what she's done in the past, but my experiences with her, only a half dozen or so of them," I admitted, "have been very positive."

"Yes," Helen said. "As have mine since she's worked at the cupcake shop."

"Georgie's being very generous when she says Angela is sweet." Vanessa patted Georgie's hand. "You know you see the best in everyone."

"Let's be honest here," Helen said. "She's always been an awkward girl. And in the past, she's made people uncomfortable. That doesn't go over well in retail or service work, and it doesn't make a girl very popular in a small town. But it also doesn't make her a murderer."

"Okay. Let's review the facts." I set my mug aside. "She's got motive, inheriting the shop sooner than later in case Catie decided at some point to remove her from the will. She's got opportunity, in the sense that she could easily have surprised or overpowered Catie."

Angela was easily five foot ten to Catie's petite five foot three or four. And Catie would have trusted her. She probably wouldn't have questioned her appearance at the shop so early, or if she had, it wouldn't have put her on guard.

"Does she have an alibi?" Helen asked. "Where was she early on Friday morning?"

"Oh, I owe her a check." I'd forgotten in all the hubbub. "Steph told me to drop a check with Angela. That she'd be in the shop over the next few days, keeping things rolling as best she could until the will is sorted out."

At Georgie and Vanessa's curious looks, Helen said, "That's right. You two have been sequestered writing. Since the estate won't be settled for some unknown period of time and Catie was estranged from her family, there's no one but the staff to handle her funeral. They started a collection to cover the costs."

"We can help with that," Vanessa said, with a sad smile. "The books are doing very well, and this is something we'd definitely like to help with."

"I can just add it to my check, if you like, and let them know it's from all of us?" I said.

Georgie named a sum to be added on their behalf and promised to drop a check by later, after she and Vanessa had gotten their words in for the day.

"While I'm there dropping off the check, I can ask her about her whereabouts and see if I can get her to talk about Catie."

Everyone agreed that was a fine idea.

"So that just leaves me to follow up with Heath Carson," Helen said cheerfully.

The objections to her comment were so pronounced that Fairmont woke from a deep sleep with a woof of surprise and joined us at the kitchen table. He nudged my hand with short, sharp jabs until I petted him and told him it was okay.

"You three shush. You've gone and scared Fairmont." Helen scowled at us, then reached over and petted him. "It's like you all have PHCS."

Post-Helen-Concussion Syndrome, meaning we were all more than a little worried that she'd go and get herself koshed on the head again, or worse. And yes, I definitely had PHCS. Georgie and Vanessa were likely more swayed by the specific circumstances, given Carson's history with domestic violence.

"I don't know about this nonsense with PH whatever," Vanessa said, then she shot me a rebellious look, "but I've seen Catie's medical records. You cannot confront that man alone."

I covered my face with my hands. Accessing medical records?

"Now, don't say it, Zella." Vanessa didn't even sound guilty, just defensive.

After giving my face a good scrub, I said, "What? That having a peek at someone's medical records is well beyond 'iffy'? It is. It's illegal."

"Well, there's illegal and there's doing book research," Georgie replied. Which made no sense at all. If your research was illegal, it was illegal, whether for a book or for your unlicensed PI work.

I turned to Georgie, intending to say as much, but the sweetly innocent expression on her face stopped me.

"You're not going to rat us out, so I'm sure it's fine." Georgie smiled, safe in the knowledge that I wouldn't be her downfall.

Fairmont rested his head in my lap.

Vanessa and Georgie were stressing me out, and I was stressing Fairmont out. Poor Fairmont.

Vanessa rolled her eyes. "No one will ever know."

Georgie whispered, "Our source is really good."

I had savings. I could front them bail money. I invited Fairmont to put his front feet on my lap so I could hug him. I needed some dog love. These ladies were going to put me on blood-pressure medication.

An armful of furry love makes everything better. And truly, what were the chances some judge would sentence these two women—women who referred to a search engine as "the Google"—to actual time in jail?

Vanessa could play up her dodgy knee (even though it was less dodgy all the time) and Georgie could just be her sweet, lovely self, and they'd probably get off with a warning. I let go of Fairmont, and he dropped his front feet back down to the floor.

Vanessa and Georgie would keep doing what they did—potentially illegal sources and all—and I'd pretend it wasn't happening. I was definitely keeping their shady dealings with their even shadier source to myself. Luke could *not* hear about it.

"The point is," Vanessa said, "Helen, you can't begin to understand how violent this man is. He put his wife in the hospital with serious injuries, and that's someone he supposedly cared for."

"Agreed. But Georgie, Vanessa, I just want to say..." I couldn't let their risky behavior go completely without comment. "There's no baking in prison, Vanessa. And Georgie, I hear the coffee is terrible. Like acid. You don't want to get thrown in the slammer."

"Untrue. About the baking," Helen declared with a conspiratorial grin pointed in Vanessa's direction. "Someone has to feed all those convicted felons."

"And you." I pointed my mom glare Helen's way.

"I will never forgive you or myself if you confront that man and he lays a finger on you."

After a little hemming and hawing, we finally all agreed that no one, none of the four of us, would dare to confront Heath Carson alone.

"So I'm off to visit Angela, and then— Oh, no." I lifted a hand to my temple and pressed two fingers there. "Please save me from middle-of-the-night promises. I told Luke I'd take care of Turbo."

Not like I'd have declined if he hadn't asked in the middle of the night, but I'd not have forgotten having made the promise.

Helen laughed. "That man knows you well enough to know that you aren't going to be in any state to handle a puppy, three-legged or otherwise, before noon. Not after you've had a night like you've had."

"No, he said he had the morning handled. I just...forgot."

"I'll take him for the day." Helen grinned. "Sounds like fun. But you'll have to walk him first. Turbo on a leash is too much for me. He's practically full grown, and that missing leg doesn't slow him down a bit."

"Deal," I agreed. "I'll pick him up, take him for a walk, then drop him at your house. And then I'll visit Angela."

"We'll be writing," Vanessa said, glancing at the

clock on my stove. "And speaking of, we need to get hopping."

As the SGG filed out of my house, I had some sense of accomplishment. Vanessa and Georgie would be busy at home writing. Granted, that wouldn't keep them from diving into virtual trouble via their dodgy "source," but it would keep them physically safe.

And better yet, Helen had a precocious puppy to keep her occupied...and homebound. I would conveniently not drop off Turbo's crate. There was no way that pup was reliable loose in a house or backyard. So she'd be stuck home until I picked him up.

The SGG were safe for the time being.

Fairmont nudged my hand.

I kneeled down and petted him. "Mission accomplished, buddy. Now we just have to save Bubba's reputation and get Catie's killer sorted out, preferably before any of the ladies do anything wildly inappropriate."

Fairmont huffed.

Maybe it was a small canine sneeze, but it sounded a lot like doggie laughter.

16

C hief Charleston had a hide-a-key.

Yes, the chief of White Sage Police had a generic, store-bought hide-a-key.

Did the man *want* his house broken into?

He and I would be having a little chat about getting a programmable lock if he was worried about Turbo alone indoors and a caretaker needing to get inside his house.

Or maybe Helen could chat with him about burying a key, versus announcing its presence with a patently fake plastic rock.

But that was a problem for another day. A day when the chief wasn't locked up for assaulting a man who'd deserved whatever Bubba Charleston had thrown at him.

Since I liked the interior of my vehicle just as it

was—unchewed—I retrieved the travel crate Luke told me was stashed in the chief's spare room. Not to be confused with the giant wire crate Turbo used as his personal palace when the chief had to leave him at home.

I looked at Turbo, waiting patiently in his monster-sized crate in the corner of the living room. "I'm coming back for you, little guy. Just give me a second to load up the car. You're as well supplied as a firstborn toddler."

He stood up when I started talking to him and tipped his head, giving me a cutely curious look. What a darling dog. I couldn't help wondering what Fairmont had looked like at that age.

After I loaded the smaller plastic crate into my Grand Cherokee, I tackled the pile of supplies Luke had arranged near the front door for me. Finally, it was time to load Turbo.

It was a complete fiasco.

Turbo failed to get the memo that he only had three legs. Also, I now knew where his name came from.

When I opened his crate door, he went from standing patiently inside to reveling in his freedom in the blink of an eye. He shot around the chief's living room like a toddler on a sugar high while I stood in the middle of it all holding his leash and hoping he'd run out of steam.

As I watched, I decided a toddler on a sugar high was preferable. At least the two-legged child ran *around* the living room and its furniture at turbo speed. The three-legged fiend I'd unleashed bounded *over* anything in his path: the coffee table, the sofa, the coffee table again, the armchair.

It took me a quarter of an hour to wrangle a leash on him. And I only finally managed it when I remembered the bag of treats that I'd loaded in the car.

Treats retrieved, I crinkled the plastic bag, sprinkled a few on the ground, and then ambushed him with the leash as he scarfed them down without chewing.

Turbo happily let me lift him into his crate and snoozed the whole way home. Of course he did— he'd exhausted himself with the nonstop victory laps he'd done in the chief's living room.

I parked in my drive and got ready to remove the Tasmanian devil from his travel crate. That was about when I decided that Bubba Charleston was going to owe me a steak.

Big, round, meltingly sweet brown eyes stared back at me when I popped the hatch on the Grand Cherokee.

I wagged a finger at him. "You're a monstrous liar."

He'd been exactly this calm and seemingly well-behaved as he'd waited patiently in his crate at home. Right up until I'd opened the crate door.

I'd already discovered that three legs were much, much faster than two. So as I eyeballed him, I decided if I wasn't going to be quicker, I had to be smarter. I resorted to bribery.

Eventually, I got him out using my body as a shield in front of the crate, opening the door only wide enough for my hand to slip in, and wedging my hip against the door as he tried to shove it open.

The stakes were high, what with the lack of four walls to contain the spotted lunatic if he escaped the crate without a leash, so I put my all into it.

Once out of the car, he hit the end of the leash, realized he'd lost this round, and sat obediently next to me.

He tilted his head as if to say, "Why are you all worked up, lady?"

I'd broken a sweat just getting him out of the car. One part hard work—keeping that door wedged just right had taken some talent—and one part nerves, since an ill-timed fumble would have resulted in me chasing a gleeful bundle of energy down the street.

"You are such a liar. Adorable and sweet, but a huge, monstrous fibber."

Those expressive, darling eyes promised angelic behavior that Turbo absolutely did not deliver.

I deposited him in the yard to give myself a

breather. And since I was a fan of correctly modeled behavior and its influence on youthful minds, I let Fairmont join him for a romp.

They hadn't met before, so I kept a close eye for the first few minutes, but they both showed signs of being nothing but completely over the moon with the other's company.

As I watched them play, I decided I'd take both of them on the walk to Helen's.

Which was how I ended with Fairmont, Turbo, and a tangle of leashes at the end of my drive a few minutes later. Helen's house was only a few streets over; I could handle one polite dog and a puppy in a special walking harness.

Five minutes later, I wasn't so sure of myself... and I'd only made it down my driveway and past the empty house next door.

"Zella!" Betsy Severs called. She stood at her adorably decorated mailbox, black with bright red ladybugs. She stashed an envelope inside, raised the flag, then waved at me.

I succumbed to Turbo's enthusiastic charge and trotted toward her.

Fairmont didn't seem bothered by Turbo's exuberance, thankfully, but that was likely in part due to the fact that he wasn't being tugged and pulled about. The occasional shoulder bump, he ignored.

I stopped just short of jumping range. Good thing, because based on the speed of his tail, a certain young pointer would have been tempted to jump on Betsy.

"I'll walk with you, if you'd like the company." Her eyes gleamed with excitement. "My new cleaner has a teenage daughter she brings with her. I slip her a few extra babysitting dollars for some alone time while the house gets cleaned. It's blissful."

I could hardly say no. Not only would I love the help, but she seemed keen to escape the house and her kids. Hers was a rowdy household.

No judgment at all. Actually, I'd go so far as to say that I'd probably be looking to escape on a much more regular basis if I was in her shoes.

"I'm headed to Helen's to drop off this rambunctious ball of fur."

"Helen's dog-sitting while the chief is, ah, not available?"

"It's a joint effort, but essentially, yes."

Betsy glanced at Turbo, who in less than a minute had wrapped himself around my legs and was in danger of permanently maiming me. Without comment, Betsy untangled us.

She handed the leash back to me. "Just give me two seconds. I'll run inside to let the hoodlums know I'll be gone for twenty minutes."

When she returned, I was rather proud of

myself. I'd managed to keep my legs free of the leash and had curbed a possible mutiny when both dogs spotted a squirrel.

"I thought taking Fairmont along might help." I followed that nonsensical comment (what had I been thinking?) with a self-deprecating roll of my eyes.

"Hm. I'll take the pup." She produced a stick of plastic-wrapped cheese from her pocket. "I even brought bribes."

Turbo levitated when he caught wind of her treat. All three legs left the ground at once, as if he'd turned into a pogo stick.

Betsy snagged the loop of the leash from me, fiddled with the harness I'd barely managed to get on Turbo until it fit correctly, then changed how the leash was attached. In a blink she had a tiny piece of cheese in her hand held low and Turbo under moderate control.

He was still a bouncy six-month-old pup, but the change was impressive.

She saw my look of complete and utter shock—she had skills, as my daughter Greta would say—and laughed. "I have three boys and am a full-time writer. I can multitask with the best of them. I also grew up with a crazy dog-lady mother. Dog shows on the weekends, training during the week."

Fairmont sat quietly at my side, and I thanked

heaven he'd been my introduction to dog ownership.

And not just because he was so well-behaved. That was only one of the reasons that Fairmont was special. One of so many. I scratched him underneath his collar.

"Ae you still writing romance and horror?" I asked.

"I just went full-time with my sports romance pen name, so I don't have much time for horror anymore, but I do like to write it." She walked forward briskly, keeping the piece of cheese near Turbo's nose and feeding him a tiny bit every so often. She grinned when she looked up and saw me watching. "If it gets me there without a dislocated shoulder, I'm calling it good."

"Oh, yes." I certainly hadn't been about to complain. "You're doing the heavy lifting on this walk. I'm nothing but appreciative."

"After you and Helen watched the kids the other night, gosh, it's the least I can do. Derek and I had a great date night. And I missed my jog this morning, because he had an early work call, so the walk is appreciated."

Jogging? Writing full-time? There'd been a shift in the Severs household, if I wasn't mistaken. "It was no trouble at all. We'd be glad to do it again. And congratulations." When she looked puzzled, I added, "On your writing."

"Oh! Yes." Her smile broadened. "I love it. We've got a part-time nanny, better babysitting options, the cleaner comes more frequently, and my husband's workday has shortened recently. He's telecommuting."

"Ah, with the boys in the house, isn't that—"

She chuckled. "Oh, he's not at the house. There is no possible way that would work. Even if we soundproofed a room and put an unpickable lock on it. My boys have ingenuity and determination oozing from their pores. I blame their father. That's what I get for marrying a genius."

I'd only met Betsy's other half in passing, but almost everything I'd heard about him made him sound like a lovely man. A hardworking one, but still very present.

"I don't suppose he's taken an office space out at The Hiker?" Geraldine's tiny home B and B community, The Hiker's Second Home, had an adjoining set of buildings she leased out as office, studio, and conference space.

"He has! He loves it. Sundays and Mondays, he's off. Tuesdays and Thursdays, he works from the shed in our backyard—which is a bit of a joke, but his employers love him, so they tolerate the boys' interruptions. And Wednesdays, Fridays, and Saturdays, he's out at Geraldine's in his office. If his office mate would just hurry up and retire, he could work out of that space five days a week."

It sounded like Betsy and her family were doing really well, which I loved hearing. Betsy and her husband had their share of past troubles, so it was especially heartwarming to see her so happy.

We walked in silence for a bit, and I watched her handle Turbo with relative ease. He was doing a good approximation of a polite dog, but he'd certainly be too much for Helen to manage. She'd been right about that.

"So, with my husband out at Geraldine's regularly now, he mentioned..." She peeked at me from the corner of her eye then quickly fed Turbo a tiny piece of cheese.

"Yes?" There were so many different directions this gossip train could take that I didn't want to even guess.

"Geraldine and the chief have been seeing a lot of each other lately."

After seeing her concern for the chief and hearing her call him "John," that wasn't a complete surprise. But just as I'd refrained from commenting to the SGG, I said nothing now for fear of stepping on the couple's possible budding relationship.

After a bit of silence, Betsy said, "I'm not sure if you know, because you're new to town, but most people in town think Luke is Bubba's son."

"I'm not sure Luke has any idea of those rumors, so—"

"Oh! I would never say anything to Luke." Her lips twisted. "He's always been really nice to me. Both Bubba and him. Some people in town aren't so kind. The chief was especially good to me when I was sorting myself out."

The Betsy Severs I knew had welcomed me to White Sage, dropped chocolates by my house when I'd been feeling down, and always had a smile and kind word for me. Though we weren't close, I absolutely considered her a friend.

I found it difficult to believe that she'd given the townsfolk any reason to be unkind...except she'd had a drinking problem a few years ago, and that part of her past had clearly left its mark on the memory of White Sage.

Impulsively, I stopped and hugged her. With our hands full of dogs, it didn't last long, but my intent was clearly conveyed. She had my support whenever she needed it.

And Fairmont's. He leaned his head against her leg until Turbo decided to jump on top of him in an effort to start a wrestling match.

We stepped away from each other to separate the dogs. Fairmont was a saint, but even he didn't particularly like being pounced on top of while attached to his human and unable to reciprocate.

When she met my gaze, her eyes held the glint of dampness. She smiled at me then picked up her brisk gait once again. After a few seconds, she said, "You know I ran into him."

"The chief?" I asked. "Or Luke?"

"Sorry. My head's bouncing around and shifting gears extra fast today. Lots of caffeine this morning. No, I ran into the guy the chief clocked."

"Heath Carson," I muttered automatically. "Really? Where?"

"Lucky's. Derek and I went for a late dinner after we put the kids down. We try to grab dinner out every week or two now that we've found a more reliable babysitter."

"You know Helen and I are happy to help out anytime you two need a break." We'd had fun. The boys had been more entertaining than we'd expected. Full of mischief but not meanness. Wait a minute... "Wasn't Lucky's the bar where the chief and Carson had their altercation?"

Although, if it had been a fight, wouldn't Carson have been locked up as well? If it hadn't been the middle of the night when I spoke with him, I liked to think I'd have had the presence of mind to get the details from the chief himself.

"Yes, except Lucky's isn't really a bar. They serve beer and wine, but it's more of a greasy spoon and barbecue place." Betsy slowed her pace, which meant she had to up Turbo's cheese reward. I suspected she wanted a few more minutes to chat, because we were coming up on Helen's street. "Derek and I must have just missed it. We passed the chief coming in on our way out."

Too bad she hadn't seen what had happened between the two men.

With the chief locked up and Carson free, either Bubba Charleston had thrown the first punch, or it hadn't been a "fight" at all. The chief's blackened eye had been a result of his arrest, not Heath Carson landing a punch.

"When you say you ran into the man the chief hit—"

"Literally. I bumped into him leaving the ladies' room. After I'd apologized, he asked if I was local. And when I said yes, he asked me for a recommendation for a place to stay in town."

Friday night—*late* Friday night—Catie's ex had been looking for a place to stay in White Sage. That made no sense. Not even a little bit. Catie had been murdered early Friday morning. What killer did the deed then hung around all day long?

I shouldn't ask where she recommended he stay, and yet... "Did you give him a recommendation?"

"Oh, sure. The Hiker's full up, what with the fishing tournament, and this guy didn't look like the type to stay in a rustic tiny-home community anyway. He was wearing a full-on three-piece suit, looked like he'd come straight from some swanky office. I figured Martha's would be more his speed and also less likely to be filled up with fishermen."

Martha had a more upscale B and B in the center of town that catered to the winery- and distillery-touring crowd.

Wonderful. Now I knew where to find Heath Carson.

I hadn't been tempted to confront him when he'd been a violent stranger, location unknown, who'd put his wife in the hospital and possibly murdered her. Now he was the man in a three-piece suit staying at the eminently civilized Rose Inn.

Guests of the Rose Inn went on wine tours, bought bourbon-cherry jam at the local distillery, and definitely didn't murder their ex-wives.

Which didn't mean I planned to meet Carson face to face...but maybe I was a tiny bit less ill at ease with the idea.

Which was ridiculous. He was still a potential murder suspect with a history of violence.

"Zella?"

We'd come to a stop in front of Helen's house, at the base of her driveway.

"Sorry. I'm just..."

"In the middle of trying to figure out who murdered Catie?" Her forehead wrinkled with worry lines. "I know. It's not like the sleuthing grannies can be stopped. At least they've got you to keep an eye on them."

I wasn't so sure Luke would agree, but since that was exactly how I saw my relationship with the feisty, independent women of the SGG, I couldn't help a broad smile in reply.

Betsy glanced at Helen's front door. "I'm gonna power-walk back to the house. I don't want to break the teenager. She's in training as our evening backup babysitter for the boys."

"Best to start in small doses," I agreed.

She paused. "Look, I don't want you to think I'm gossiping." She glanced heavenward. "Of course I'm gossiping, but it's coming from a good place, I swear."

I nodded enthusiastically. Betsy was no vicious spreader of untrue tales.

"I wanted you to know about Geraldine and Bubba, I don't know, just in case Luke didn't know. It's going to get back to him, and better it come from someone who cares. What with the two of them getting closer, well, that might create more talk about...other things."

"Like who Luke's real dad is," I said wryly.

"Yeah." As Turbo started to fidget, she shoveled the remaining cheese into his mouth. "You'll let me know if there's anything I can do for Bubba? I don't have any idea what that man could have done to set him off, but the chief is good people. I just, I didn't really know who to offer my help to."

I forgot that Betsy and Derek weren't local to the area. Hence the lack of readymade relatives to babysit. She'd been here several years, but she wasn't a local.

I looked pointedly at Turbo. "I think you've already done a lot. I'm not sure how long I'll have this crazy little guy." Which we both knew meant I hadn't a clue how long the chief would be locked up. "So if you want to stretch your legs again, let me know. I'd love the company—and the canine expertise doesn't hurt."

I took the leash from her and assured her I could manage up the driveway alone.

I managed to keep the dogs from tangling with each other or me on my way to Helen's front door, even though my head was spinning.

Late on Friday night, Carson had been dressed for the office and looking for a hotel room. Which sounded a lot like the actions of a man just arriving in town after leaving his posh office job in Dallas.

That still didn't explain his presence in town after his ex-wife's murder, but it also didn't support him as a suspect.

Could he have come to town earlier? Sometime before Catie's death early on Friday morning?

And if he'd come to town previously and murdered his ex in a fit of rage, would he have stuck around? Found a place to stay? Been dressed for work?

Unless Heath Carson was putting on an elaborate show, he'd driven to White Sage from Dallas, coming directly from work without even stopping at home to change. Then he found a local place to eat dinner and gotten a recommendation for local accommodations.

And *then* he'd been assaulted by our very own chief of police.

You'd have to be a lunatic to put on that kind of show. You just killed someone; you'd leave town. Simple as that.

Did that mean that Carson was no longer my number one suspect?

I wanted to know more about his movements, but I didn't want to confront the man. He was dangerous.

And besides, I had a pressing appointment with another suspect. I needed to drop off a check with Angela—and ask some questions.

I knocked on Helen's door. Time to deposit the distraction that would keep Helen out of the mix for the remainder of the day. She opened the door as I was expressing my thanks to the bouncy three-legged dog at my side.

17

My handoff with Helen was as fast as I could possibly manage it.

Lying wasn't a skill I'd ever mastered, and while I was excellent at keeping secrets, I was less adept at keeping the fact of a secret under wraps. One good look at me and Helen would know I had information on our latest case.

But Heath Carson was dangerous, and I was trying to keep Helen and the other SGG ladies' involvement limited to murder meetings. The legwork was up to me, which meant keeping my newfound information under my hat.

With all of this in mind, I finagled a lightning-fast handoff and was out the door before Helen could do much more than acknowledge Fairmont and take Turbo's leash. I almost forgot the tug and chew toys I'd stuffed in my pockets.

"When will you be back?" Helen asked my back.

Over my shoulder, I called, "After I've dropped off my check with Angela and checked in with the chief."

"But—"

"Call you later!" I said as I hoofed it down her driveway. She'd have angled for an invite to see the chief if I'd lingered even a heartbeat longer. "Good boy, Fairmont."

He trotted alongside me, looking pleased as punch. Why wouldn't he be? He'd gotten to play with Turbo in the backyard and then divested himself of the bouncy youngster before he'd become too much of a nuisance.

"He's best in small doses, isn't he?"

Fairmont's nose tipped toward me for a split second, acknowledging my voice, but he had important business to handle. Now that the distraction of Turbo's constant jostling and nudging was gone, he could get down to the good stuff: sniffing the smells and eyeing the critter action.

And yet he was ever the gentleman. My heart hurt, because his beautiful behavior reminded me of his past, which reminded me that our relationship might not be as permanent as I liked. I hadn't checked my email today. What with my unexpected guests this morning and Catie's death weighing on my mind, that was no surprise. But mostly I just hadn't made time, because I didn't want bad news.

"We're not borrowing trouble. We're going to assume the best until we know otherwise."

This time, he stopped and looked up at me, staring as if he was waiting for something.

I kneeled and hugged him. How did he always know when I was upset? My voice, my scent, something clued him in to my distress, and there he was, all warm and furry and full of love.

With a final squeeze, I let him go. "Are you the best dog?"

He wagged his tail in response.

"Let's go drop off this check with Angela and then we can stop by lockup and chat with the chief. He'll probably get a kick out of our Turbo adventures."

Fairmont wagged his tail faster. His spotted butt swayed as his tail speed increased.

Even if he wasn't mine forever, I was lucky to have him in my life now.

The future can't steal the past, as I'd told myself so many times before.

Just because my ex-husband turned out to be a philandering ass, that didn't change the memories I had of him when he'd been completely and utterly in love with me. And it didn't take away the love I'd had for him.

If Fairmont didn't get to stay with me, so be it. I'd always have these memories, these feelings, this time.

And with those thoughts, I'd reached my daily allowed allotment of introspection. Fairmont and I hoofed it home, me getting a little exercise by walking at a very fast clip, and Fairmont content to trot by my side and experience the wonders of the outside world.

An hour later, I was pulling into a parking space directly in front of Catie's. The parking gods had most certainly smiled, because Main Street was hopping. Typical for an early Saturday afternoon in White Sage.

An odd sound from the back had me looking over my shoulder. If I didn't know better, I'd say that Fairmont had growled.

Fairmont rarely growled, and if he had been, he wasn't any longer. I turned off my radio just to be sure, but silence followed.

I glanced back to find all the hair on his back standing up. His neck was stretched forward, his head slowly pivoting as he tracked something in front of the car.

Following his line of sight, I turned to the entry of Catie's where a tallish, attractive man held the door open for Steph. She had her hands full carrying two cloth grocery bags. Someone had preceded her into the store, but I couldn't identify who.

Glancing between Fairmont and the store entry, I couldn't pinpoint exactly when his hair settled flat against his back, but it was certainly at least a few seconds after the door had closed behind the stranger. His attention, however, remained completely engaged.

He continued to watch the front door with an alert expression and didn't twitch a muscle.

I hadn't a clue what to make of his behavior. He hadn't barked, and I wasn't entirely sure if he'd growled. With the radio playing, any sound he'd made had been masked. He could have sneezed, coughed, barked once quietly, or made any of a number of canine sounds.

The raised hackles were difficult to dismiss. That meant something; I just didn't know what.

After a minute or two passed without anyone entering or exiting the store, Fairmont's intent focus and rigid posture relaxed. He turned his head to find me staring at him and wagged his tail. When I didn't offer up pets immediately, he curled himself into the dog bed I kept in the back of the Grand Cherokee.

To say I was unsettled by his behavior was an understatement. I was also intensely curious as to both the identity of the man who'd held the door for

Steph and the person who'd preceded her into the shop.

Only one way I was going to find out. "Be back in a few minutes."

Fairmont didn't even blink. He was accustomed to sleeping in the back of the SUV. He enjoyed car rides so much that I didn't have the heart to leave him at home when he could join me on my errands. And when he couldn't, I still brought him along if the weather was suitable to leave him in the car.

I double-checked that all of the windows were already cracked at an appropriate height—low enough for airflow, high enough to prevent a squirrel-induced escape attempt—then headed inside.

"Zella," Steph called out as I entered. "Good to see you again."

Her eyes were overbright, almost frantic, and her glance shifted between me and...the man who'd held the door for Steph, who appeared to be having a heated argument with Angela.

My phone was out of my pocket and in my hand without any conscious thought on my part. I glanced down at it long enough to pull up Luke's number, but I didn't call. Not yet.

Phone behind my back, I walked up to Angela and the stranger, whose identity I was fairly sure I knew.

Angela's face was bright pink, and her eyes flashed with temper.

The man didn't look nearly as agitated. If anything, he looked...tired? Sad? His clothes were immaculate and expensive, his jaw stubble-free, but his eyes were ringed with dark circles.

"I'm just trying to do the right thing," he said as I stopped next to Angela.

"We don't need your help." Angela's gaze slid to me, then she tacked on a very reluctant "But thank you."

"Hi, Angela." I smiled, trying to smooth over a tense situation, but I didn't get within smacking distance of the man whose help Angela was declining, and I reminded myself that Luke was just a phone call away. "I have a check for you." With my free hand, I reached into my back pocket and pulled out the check. Surreptitiously watching the man I suspected was Carson, I handed her the check and said, "For Catie's funeral."

And there was most definitely a reaction to my comment. A strong flash of emotion. I just wasn't sure what kind. Anger? Grief?

His jaw tightened, then he looked at me, holding eye contact. "I'm Catie's ex-husband. I'd very much like to cover the costs of the funeral."

Courage in hand, I replied calmly, "I'm not sure

that's what she would have wanted, or what's best for her friends here in White Sage."

Say what you will about funerals being a deceased person's send-off to a better place, it was also equally, if not more, about the friends and family left behind. And Catie had left a town full of friends behind.

Carson's nostrils flared. Again, anger or grief? He clenched his jaw as if he was biting back words.

"This town thought very well of Catie, and this town is willing to pay for her funeral." And then I saw it: the gleam of moisture in his eyes. The man was doing his best not to cry. "Let us do this for her. Please."

He nodded. One tense jerk of his head.

Angela opened her mouth, probably to tell this guy where he could go, so I stopped her with a hand on her arm, then I pocketed my phone. "Heath?"

He nodded.

"I'm Zella." I didn't extend my hand. "I'm stopping for lunch next door, and you're coming with me."

It wasn't really an invitation. He needed to leave Catie's Cupcakery, and if that meant I was taking him with me to lunch, so be it.

He blinked, clearly surprised.

Before he could decline, I walked out the door and hoped that he followed me.

He did, which was two wins. I wanted him out of the shop, and I wanted to see Fairmont's reaction to him.

I pulled my keys from my pocket and clicked them, as if making certain the doors were locked. The sound had Fairmont out of his dog bed in a flash.

I watched as Fairmont spotted me, wagged his tail...and did nothing out of the ordinary at all.

Did we pass the car too quickly?

Was he still half-asleep?

Or had his earlier reaction been triggered by someone other than Carson?

I was fairly certain Angela had been the only one in the shop besides Steph. Unless maybe Miles had been in the back? I couldn't be sure who, if anyone, had walked into the store in front of Carson and Steph. I hadn't been watching the storefront; my eyes had been on Fairmont and his raised hackles.

Carson followed me into Sally's Sandwich Shoppe, holding the door for me after I'd opened it. He seemed to be on autopilot, dazed. Because he'd killed his wife and was consumed by guilt? Or because someone close to him had died unexpectedly and under terrible circumstances?

I approached the counter to find Sally taking orders today.

She eyed the two of us with curiosity but no

animosity. If she did know about Catie's history, then she didn't recognize Heath Carson as the past Catie had fled when she moved here.

Since it seemed Luke and I were probably still dating—even though we'd gotten into a pretty stout argument night before last—and this might look like a date to the wrong set of eyes, I indicated Carson and said, "This is Catie's ex-husband, Heath Carson."

I kept an eye on her reaction.

"I'm sorry for your loss. Catie was a good friend. We'll miss her. *I'll* miss her." She cleared her throat. "What can I get for you?"

She'd tensed, but she hadn't read him the riot act. Knowing Sally, if she knew Carson had treated Catie poorly, she'd have told him to get out of her shop. But I had to wonder if she suspected.

I shared a glance with her, and she nodded that she was okay. For now. This was the first time I'd seen her since Catie's death, but she had to know that the SGG was meddling.

Carson and I ordered then took the one available seat, a small table on the path to the restrooms.

He looked around. "Popular place."

But I wasn't interested in polite chitchat. "How did you find out about her death?" I asked.

The timeline needed clarifying. He could hardly

be her killer if he could prove definitively that he was elsewhere when the murder happened.

"I got a call midmorning yesterday from the sheriff. McCord." He leaned his forearms on the table.

"Luke McCord. He's handling the case."

"He wanted an accounting of my whereabouts early that morning." His head dropped, and I could see a flush of red spread along the back of his neck. "I was alone. I head into work late on Fridays, so I slept in. I always sleep alone these days."

I didn't know what to say to that. It was a strange detail to share...unless one knew his background.

He looked up and met my eyes. "You know."

This man had a terrible temper. Or worse, could be coldly, brutally violent. Whatever his underlying temperament, he was capable of violence.

But I was in a public place, surrounded by people who would never let him lay a finger on me. So, I replied honestly. "Not everything."

"Some of it. That I hurt her." His face and neck were flushed an angry red, but his shoulders weren't tense with imminent violence.

If I was reading him right, what I was seeing wasn't anger. It was shame.

I bit my lip and nodded. What could I say? He beat his wife. There was little I found more reprehensible.

Murder, of course, but I was having serious doubts that this man had anything to do with Catie's death. If he took Luke's call in Dallas the morning of the murder, he couldn't have done it. It had to be a four, maybe five-hour drive. Luke would be in a position to verify his alibi. For now, I had to take him at his word.

He laughed and looked heavenward. There was no humor in the sound, only pain and shame.

When he looked back at me, his lip curled with distaste. For himself, if I was right in my reading of him thus far. "My dad wanted to put *me* in the hospital after he found out what happened." He pinched the bridge of his nose hard, touching the moist corners of his eyes with finger and thumb. When he looked up, he looked gutted. "My dad's a really nice guy. Not violent. I didn't even know he knew how to throw a punch."

I didn't know what to say. I wasn't his therapist. I had no advice. And I certainly wasn't here to make him feel better. "Can you blame him?"

A huge breath whooshed from his lungs. "No." After an emotionally fraught silence, he said in a very small voice for such a big man, "Was she happy here?"

That I could answer. I remembered the society pictures we'd found and how they'd compared to the

Catie we'd come to know. "I truly believe that she was."

Our food arrived, putting an end to this terrible conversation. I should probably eat, but I had no appetite. "I'm sorry, Sally, but could I get this to go?" I asked.

Sally's eyes were huge. I could only imagine what she must think. I'd been sitting across from a distraught man, probably appearing to grill him and bringing him to the brink of tears.

Carson had pushed his plate away as well.

When she indicated it was no problem, I said, "His as well, I think."

She nodded then disappeared with both plates.

"You'll let Angela and the staff handle Catie's funeral?"

His jaw tensed. "I just want to help. Money isn't an issue."

"You understand it's not about the money? It's about letting us take care of someone we cared about."

His eyes burned. "Yes. I understand that," he responded tightly.

"This is about Catie and the people here who love her." *And that's not you* was implied, even if I didn't say the words.

He nodded. "I'll stay. In case there's any way I can help."

Perhaps I had a mercenary streak. Or I was more of an opportunist than I'd realized, because what came out of my mouth next was downright diabolical and certainly leveraging this man's emotional state. But I was okay with that.

"Create a scholarship."

"What?"

"In Catie's honor. She was intent on giving the people around her a second chance." Which was true. According to Miles, he and Angela were "White Sage losers," but Catie hadn't seen them that way.

And then there was Liam. The encouragement with community college that he'd described Catie giving him had likely sparked the scholarship idea.

Good job, subconscious.

"Yeah. I can do that." He rubbed his forehead. "Anonymously, of course, because…"

Because what better way to taint the scholarship than to have it come out that the funds originated with a man Catie had changed her entire identity to escape?

Which prompted me to add, "In her new name."

"Yes." He pulled out his phone and made a few notes.

And while I had him in a charitable place… "Our chief of police is currently being held pending charges for assault."

Carson looked up from his phone with a hard look in his eyes. "I told him I was just here to help."

"You know that one of the first things Catie did when she moved here was to check in with Sheriff McCord and Chief Charleston? She wanted them to know about her background, just in case she had any problems crop up from her past." I met his angry look head-on.

He looked away first.

"And what twenty-something girl has a will?"

It was a rhetorical question.

But he answered me. "Twenty-seven. She was twenty-seven, not a girl. And probably a woman who knows what it's like to fear for her life." He scrubbed his hands across his face. "I'll call the sheriff. I'll make it right."

That was Chief Charleston's problem solved, I hoped.

He'd been a good part of the reason that the SGG had gotten involved, and yet... I couldn't just walk away. Not now.

Not when I'd involved myself emotionally with the outcome of the investigation.

Not when Fairmont had given me what I was almost certain was a clue.

I needed to have that chat with Angela.

18

B efore Carson and I parted, I suggested he stay
out of sight until the funeral.

I might have threatened him with the mighty
sword of White Sage gossip.

Thus far, the only locals who knew about his
history with Catie were Luke and the chief (they
weren't talking to anyone) and the SGG (who'd stay
mum if I asked). I might have implied rumors were
more likely to fly if he was seen out and about in
town.

And by implied, I mean that I stated it quite
clearly.

I stopped by the car to check on Fairmont and
found him deeply asleep atop his bed in the back.
He was sprawled dead-bug style with his four feet in
the air and his head thrown back.

It seemed like it would be an uncomfortable position, but he appeared blissfully happy, so I left him to his slumber. I deposited my lunch on the hood of the car near the windshield. I didn't expect to be long, and outside of a desire not to wake Fairmont, I didn't trust him alone with my lunch in an enclosed vehicle. He was a gentleman, but he was still a dog.

Then it was time to tackle Angela. I squared my shoulders and headed once again for Catie's Cupcakery.

I should probably invent a reason for my return visit, since I'd already delivered the check I'd promised. Luke could always use some cupcakes. If he'd had his fill of sweets, he'd just share them at work.

Decision made, I entered the shop to the tinkling of the door's bells. The sweet scents of baked goods and icing greeted me.

This time there were a few customers in line ahead of me. Only Angela was behind the counter, so I hoped that Steph was in the back or that there'd be a lull long enough for me to slip Angela a few questions.

After I'd come to the front of the queue twice and ceded my spot to the person in line behind me a second time, Angela hit me with one of her no-nonsense looks and said, "You want to talk."

"If Steph can cover for you?"

She leaned closer and said quietly, "Steph went home. She wasn't looking so good, and since we serve food, we're careful about illness. Probably just upset about Catie, but you can't be too careful. Miles got here about five minutes ago, though." She turned and called over her shoulder, "Miles! Need you up front."

"Heya, Zella," Miles said when he spotted me. "Thanks. You know, for the other night. Luke was really cool about the, ah, you know, that thing I did."

Mentoring a delinquent vandal and vandalizing property were "that thing I did." How minimalist of him. "No problem. Happy I could help."

He grinned. "It's good to have an in with the coppers, right?"

"If I did that *thing you do*, it probably would be, Miles."

He shrugged, looking not the least bit repentant. It looked like White Sage wasn't about to be deprived of its urban art after all. Luke was a softy.

"Miles, can you box up Zella's order and put it to the side for her? We're going to talk in the back for a bit." Angela gestured to the back office.

After ordering an assorted dozen, I followed Angela.

As soon as I'd closed the door behind me, she

said, "You want to know where I was early Friday morning."

More direct than I'd have been, but since I *did* want to know if she had an alibi, I replied, "If you don't mind telling me."

"I know how White Sage is. You've probably heard twenty stories about what a terrible person I am and also that I'm in line to inherit the Cupcakery."

"I haven't." When her no-nonsense gaze drilled into mine, I added, "Yes, I had heard that you were in Catie's will, but that's not anything that won't be public knowledge as soon as her attorney is made aware of her passing."

Angela's mouth firmed into a grim line. "Her murder. She didn't 'pass'. Someone murdered her. Catie was the last person, really, the very last person anyone would ever want to hurt." Her eyes flashed with some deep emotion. "People like you don't get it."

I didn't like where this was headed. I hadn't asked any rude or prying questions. I might have gotten around to it, but I hadn't yet. And still she was attacking, pointing a figurative finger at me, like I was something less than.

"I don't know what you mean." Even though I was fairly sure I did.

"You're rich. You're gorgeous. Have you ever had

to work for anything in your life? Have you ever been at the bottom of the heap?"

The cruelty of those words cut me, because I'd been at the bottom of a few heaps—just not the same ones she was referencing.

I didn't know how to respond, how to deflect from my own troubles, because I was too stunned by the accusation and where it sent me mentally. I didn't want to revisit those bottom-of-the-heap moments. Not in the office of a recently murdered woman with a potential suspect only feet away.

"Oh, God." Angela collapsed into the chair behind the desk. She bent her head, then rested her forehead in her palms. When she looked up, her eyes were red. But dry. She wasn't going to cry. Not now, not in front of me. "I'm sorry. You don't deserve that. You've never been anything but nice to me."

"Not that this is the time or the place to discuss it, but everyone has their troubles, Angela. Everyone. Sometimes they just look a little different than the ones we've experienced ourselves." I blinked. "But you're right. I've been very fortunate in many ways, and I try not to forget that."

"Catie would be ashamed of me."

"I doubt that very much." And I meant it. Catie had been on the side of the underdog, as I'd learned only these last few days. She'd been the giver of second chances. She understood what it was like to be knocked back in life and to start over again.

Angela sniffed and dabbed the tip of her nose with a tissue. "Okay, you want an alibi. Like I told the police, Catie had planned to start earlier than usual on Friday. She was working on filling a big order that needed to be delivered Friday evening for a Saturday party. From there, it's simple enough to calculate the timeline. Assuming she started at four thirty, and taking into account the number of cupcakes she'd completed, she was, ah... She was interrupted some-time after six."

I must have made some kind of noise, because she stopped and looked at me with an expression of concern.

If Angela truly was a suspect—and as the person who'd benefit the most financially, she was—then I likely shouldn't trust her math.

I didn't want to trust her math.

Her math placed Catie's death mere minutes before Helen and I had arrived. If we'd been as little as fifteen or twenty minutes earlier, we might have saved Catie's life.

Or been injured ourselves.

When I didn't comment, she continued, "I started an early-morning yoga class recently."

Yoga wasn't my preferred method of exercise, but

to each their own. When she didn't elaborate, I raised my eyebrows in question.

She gave me a wry look. "Yoga's supposed to chill you, right? Not so much for me, but Catie recommended it, said it helped her keep a clear mind, so I committed to a six-week class, to give it a solid effort, you know? I go a few times a week. Catie handles— handled—most of the early-morning baking. I only come in early when we're booked full up with party orders and then once a week so Catie got a real day off."

"What time does your yoga class start?"

"Six on the nose, and the instructor wants us there at least five minutes before class. I'm not a morning person, so I give myself a little extra time."

I didn't reply immediately, because I was taking it all in: whether I could trust Angela's conclusion that Catie's baking was interrupted around six, how close Helen's and my arrival was to Catie's death and the various implications of that startling discovery, what kind of person gets up obscenely early to attend a class she clearly doesn't enjoy—

"I can do this," Angela said. "I'm not a morning person, but I can get up early to bake. And the customers... I can do this."

Since I had no idea what prompted her outburst —was honestly too upset about the implications of the timeline to even guess—I said, "I never said otherwise."

She chewed her lip as she watched me. Eventually she said, "Running the shop. Baking the cupcakes. Catie believed I could do it. She told me she had faith in me."

I closed my eyes and touched my temple. I could feel the pounding of my own pulse there, a good indicator that a headache wasn't far off. When I opened my eyes, I found her staring, waiting for some kind of response. "I'm sure that's true."

She tilted her head, and some of the tension in her shoulders eased. "You found her."

"I did." I pressed my lips together and swallowed the excess saliva that pooled in my mouth. My stomach churned unpleasantly. I would not be sick. I hadn't been when Fairmont found Catie, and I wouldn't be now.

She let out a loud exhale and then stretched out her neck. "You just want to know where I was. You're not accusing me of anything or telling me I can't run the Cupcakery like Catie."

She wasn't asking. She was verbalizing for the sake of clarity (her own), not to dispel any misconceptions between us.

"Catie's one of the few people to have faith in me. I can get..."

"Defensive?"

"Yeah." She scribbled on a notepad, yanked the note free, and handed it to me. "My yoga instructor. I've already given her name and number to the police, but feel free to call her. If you're interested, she's got spaces in her morning yoga class."

I recognized the name on the sheet, Rachelle Anderson, Vanessa and Helen's personal trainer. That made confirmation of Angela's alibi easier, since I could have one those ladies call her for a chat.

Angela had an alibi. Yes, I'd need to verify it, but I suspected that Luke had already done that and excluded her. Too bad Luke and I couldn't exactly share notes. Or rather, too bad he couldn't share his notes, because I certainly shared everything I learned.

I hesitated to end the conversation. Not because I needed anything else from Angela, simply because my legs didn't want to move.

My rear was glued to the chair.

I was so tired.

"If you hadn't found her, I would have," Angela said into the awkward silence.

I looked up and focused on her; it took a little effort. Her eyes were huge and serious in her face. Still red, still dry.

"I wasn't scheduled, but I planned to come in

after yoga and give her a hand with the rest of the party order and start the day's baking."

"You wouldn't have..." I gathered myself and finished my thought. "She wasn't here. Fairmont found her in the dentist's parking lot."

"Still. I don't think I could have handled it. Not like you have. I'm glad it was you."

I didn't know how to respond. I thought I knew what she meant, but I didn't know what to say, so I lifted the note she'd given me with a small smile of thanks and left.

I'd have walked out the door without my cupcakes if Miles hadn't caught me at the door and shoved the box into my hands. He squeezed my arm, then opened the door for me.

It took me a good several minutes sitting in the driver's seat before I had my head on straight and was ready to drive home. The last thing Fairmont or I needed was to be involved in a car accident because I wasn't driving safely.

And I really wanted to take a nap.

Or a vacation.

From a life where I had few responsibilities and no job.

I sighed. I was emotionally exhausted, my blood sugar was likely low, and I'd just lost my last suspect.

Maybe, if I'd been thinking a little more clearly, I'd have taken time to reevaluate my suspect list.

Fairmont abandoned his comfortable bed and his favorite car-riding activity (pressing his nose to the crack in the window and experiencing all the scents the world had to offer) in favor of resting his chin on my shoulder.

We spent the ride home that way: me focusing all of my energy on driving and not dwelling, and Fairmont with his chin nuzzled next to my ear.

The car smells of ham and cheese and makes my mouth water.

It smells of butter and flour and sugar. I really like butter and flour and sugar. Zella doesn't let me eat her cookies and cakes very often. Maybe this time?

But then the car fills with the smell of sadness. Sadness is the worst. It's all sharp and salty and makes we want to cuddle my lady.

Zella shouldn't be sad. She's warmth and light and love. She should never be sad.

I do my best to cheer her up. I let her know I'm here and I love her.

I wish Luke was here.

He makes everything better.

A knock at my door woke me from the snooze Fairmont and I had both fallen into on the couch. We don't watch much television, but I needed the distraction.

And the cuddle.

He usually waited for an invitation to join me on the sofa. But not this time. I sat down, and he was curled up next to me before I could blink.

I'd swear he was psychic if I didn't know better.

"It's me, Zella," Luke called from the other side of the door.

Which was excellent news. I couldn't face the SGG or Geraldine right now. I hadn't updated any of them on my progress today. Yet. I definitely had plans to, after I grabbed a nap.

As I extricated myself from my couch, a fuzzy

blanket, and a cuddly dog, I glanced at the dark street outside my window. Hopefully it wasn't after seven. That was when Helen and I had agreed I'd pick up Turbo. By text, naturally, because I hadn't been ready to rehash the day with her. She couldn't so easily pick up on hidden secrets by text.

At least Vanessa and Georgie were both too busy racing toward their deadline to pay house calls.

When I opened the door, Luke did a double take. "Are you okay?"

Which was when I realized I might not look so great. Instead of feeling self-conscious that I was less than presentable, I grinned and said, "I'm fine, just catching up on some lost sleep. This is what you get when you drop by unannounced."

Then I hugged him, so he'd know he was welcome whether he was announced or not.

The terrible drag of exhaustion I'd been feeling had faded with my nap, and with Luke's arms around me, I felt even better. I didn't deal well with high levels of stress and extreme emotions without sufficient amounts of sleep, and Geraldine's nocturnal visit had put a dent in my regular eight hours.

Luke stepped back when Fairmont shoved his nose between us. Kneeling in front of my suddenly pushy dog, he said, "I called. And texted."

I really was terrible about hearing my phone.

Then again, I'd been asleep, so it wasn't surprising. "What time is it?"

"Dinnertime, I hope. Are you up for some delivery pizza?" He scratched Fairmont's chest, then moved to the itchy spot under his collar, and then to his wiggling rear.

I did a quick check-in with myself and realized that I could definitely eat. "That sounds amazing. You want me to order?"

"No, I'll take care of it. Thin crust, light on the cheese, veggie?"

That was my guy. He knew my pizza order and didn't even tease.

Not to say he'd be joining me in my vegetarian option, but he'd jumped on board the "cheese is a flavoring, not a main course" bandwagon once he'd tried my thin-crust, half-cheese favorite. It wasn't exactly healthy, but it was slightly healthier than the pan, extra cheese with pepperoni that I was fairly certain he used to order. *And* it was really tasty.

"I'll just freshen up while you order."

He nodded, phone already at his ear.

Fairmont hesitated, clearly torn as to who he should shadow. I loved that my dog was so in love with Luke. It was adorable. I lifted a hand in the classic "stay" gesture and then spent the next few minutes erasing the last of my sleep fog.

I also grabbed my phone. I had several notifications, including a text from Helen saying not to worry about picking up Turbo. I guessed they'd really hit it off.

When I returned to the living room, Luke was off the phone and waiting for me on my couch. "I got an interesting call today."

"Oh?" I reviewed the day's events and considered who might have ratted out my activities to Luke. Not that I wasn't going to share everything I'd learned, but—

"You can stop looking like a caged rabbit. It was a good call...mostly. Heath Carson called and insisted he'd swear on a stack of Bibles that the chief didn't hit him."

"Ah." Not exactly what I'd expected when I discussed the chief's situation with Carson. "That's good news, right?"

"Doesn't make all the witnesses go away, but ADAs don't like to prosecute without the victim's cooperation. Carson took it a step further and said he threw a punch at the chief. Bit of a problem, since he's lying, there are witnesses to prove it, and if he had, it's a serious crime to assault a law officer."

"So...not good news?"

"Hmm. Let's just say complicated. But we'll sort it out, and I can't see Bubba losing his job over the mess now. Given how much this town loves him, and Carson's statement, he should be fine."

I had an uncomfortable feeling that now might be the time to bring up the gossip circulating about Luke and his possible parentage. I didn't want to tell him something that might only not be true, but also could harm his relationship with a man he respected and worked with. But I also didn't want him caught off guard if someone else let it slip.

"What has you looking so worried? I thought you'd be glad to hear about Bubba." He gave me a knowing look. "And Turbo. Bubba's already made arrangements to pick him up from Helen, so he won't have to overnight here."

Small favors. Although I'd planned for a romp in the yard, followed by a walk—just Turbo, me, and a lot of cheese—followed by another romp in the yard. The hope had been he'd crash out all night long in his crate, and the destruction of my house would be avoided.

"Oh, I am glad. Definitely. And as for Heath Carson's sudden about-face...I had a word with him." When I saw the dark look on Luke's face, I quickly added, "In a very public place, of course. I encouraged him to help out the chief if he could."

"Hmm." He leaned back in my sofa and crossed his ankles. I could practically read his mind. He was clearly debating the pros and cons of calling me out for that meeting.

"I was careful, Luke, I promise."

He regarded me with a serious expression and eventually nodded. "Okay."

That had been easier than I'd expected, but maybe now wasn't the greatest time to discuss the gossip about his origins and how it periodically flared to life, especially when he was arresting his presumed biological father.

"And there's that worried look again. What's going on?"

"Ah. Well, it's about some gossip, which could be like a lot of White Sage gossip and just a bunch of nonsense, but I was thinking that maybe it would come up and someone might say something to you and so—"

"Zella."

I looked up. I'd been avoiding eye contact as I gathered up the courage to drop a bomb on his personal life.

I inhaled deeply. "Fine. There's speculation that Bubba Charleston is your biological father."

First his eyes crinkled, then his lips spread in a huge smile. "You were worried how I'd feel about that."

"Well, yes. I didn't expect this." I waved a hand at his grinning mug.

"John Charleston is almost definitely my biological father."

My jaw dropped. One, he knew about the

rumors. Two, he wasn't freaked out. Three, he obviously hadn't confronted either the chief or his mom, because if he had, well, then he'd know for sure, wouldn't he?

He leaned forward and planted a soft kiss on my lips. It was over before it had even begun, but it put a stop to my gaping.

"I suspected a long time ago. My mom has more animosity for him than anyone should for an ex-boyfriend. I figured there had to be an ongoing cause. Either to do with me or her feelings for him, maybe both. And then there were the rumors." He flashed a crooked grin. "It's adorable you think I wouldn't have gotten wind of them before now."

"Well..."

He had a great point. White Sage gossip raged all around him, and as the sheriff, he had a particular interest in staying abreast. And yet no one seemed to have realized that he'd caught on to the gossip about him.

"Also, I can do simple math. I know when Bubba and my mom broke up. I know when my mom married my dad. Clearly I knew when I was born, and I also know that I look more like Bubba than my dad."

"And you're not upset?"

He shrugged. "I was, a long time ago. But they're adults and have their reasons for keeping it to themselves. I didn't understand that when I was younger, and now I do. I don't really agree with it, but why wave the choice in their face? When they're ready, they'll tell me."

"And what, you'll act all shocked and surprised?"

"No, I'll probably hug my mom and thump Bubba, and then tell them I've known for ages."

He was still kicked back casually on my sofa. He had to be exhausted. He'd been up longer than I had, and when I'd seen him at his office, I could tell the case was getting to him.

"You seem..."

He raised his eyebrows, waiting for me to finish.

"I don't know. You seem good."

"I'm fairly certain Bubba is keeping his job—something I wasn't so confident of last night—I'm sitting in my girlfriend's living room waiting for an amazing pizza to arrive, and I'm making progress on the case." He reached out and intertwined his fingers with mine. "That's enough for now."

"So I'm your girlfriend?" I asked. Because we'd never actually had that conversation. Yes, Luke had asked to meet my kids, and that seemed like a step beyond just dating.

Luke shot me an amused but quizzical look. "I'm not sure what you mean."

"We've never discussed what we are. What we're doing."

"Because *you* don't like those conversations." Luke scooted closer as Fairmont chose that moment to jump up onto the sofa next to him. "I've tried to move the conversation in that direction before, and you've always shut it down."

True. Relationships were hard. They were time-consuming and hard work and required prioritizing someone other than myself.

I'd done a lot of prioritizing of others in my life.

Then again, Luke made everything so easy. And if I was honest with myself, I loved him. I knew I did, and maybe it was cowardly of me to not admit it, even to myself, until now. But I did.

Loving Luke was easy. It was simple. It was effortless.

Even in the beginning with my ex, it hadn't been like this, and we'd been young and optimistic and ready to fall in love.

I was a complete idiot and a coward. I'd found something amazing with a wonderful man, but I'd been too cowardly to venture into the realm of new and untested emotions.

Maybe it was time to step up.

Say it out loud.

Be the first to take that step.

And the funny thing? I wasn't even being brave. It just felt right.

"I love you."

He pulled me against his side, hugged me with one arm, and kissed my temple. "I love you too." Then he leaned back and waited till I met his gaze to add, "And yes, we're dating. Exclusively."

Which made me grin. "Good. That's good. I wasn't sure after that fight the other day."

He chuckled. "That wasn't a fight, Zella."

"I'm pretty sure it was."

"You disagreed with me."

I waited for him to explain. When he didn't, I thought back on that night.

I'd mentioned Greta's pregnancy and how I planned to visit her soon. He'd expressed interest in meeting both Greta and Mark.

I'd said no, that it wasn't a good time.

He'd asked why.

I'd told him.

He'd been annoyed with my answer, which in retrospect I understood. I'd been defending my incredibly bratty and selfish children when they hadn't deserved it. Just because my kids were great ninety percent of the time, that didn't mean I should defend them the remaining ten. Even if my daughter was pregnant with her first child and very emotional.

Then he'd left, still annoyed that I didn't want him to meet my kids.

And I'd assumed we'd had a massive argument, because Luke didn't get his way.

But Luke wasn't my ex, and it wasn't fair to either of us when I behaved as if he were.

Finally, I looked at him and said, "Not a fight."

"Nope." He grinned. "You'll know without any doubts or reservations if we have an actual fight. But failing that, you can always ask."

I could just imagine how that would play out. In the midst of an emotionally trying event, I'd stop and say, "Hon, are we fighting right now?"

But he was right. I had to get better at speaking my fears, sharing my emotions, being a little vulnerable. I'd made a pretty darn good start tonight, so I figured it was worth repeating. "I love you."

The joy I saw in his eyes and the accompanying smile were worth it.

Fairmont was so wrapped up watching us cuddle and share our feelings that he flinched and woofed in surprise when the pizza delivery boy knocked on the door.

And that made Luke and me laugh.

With everything that had happened over the last two days, we both needed the release of laughter.

And we both needed pizza.

This evening had been a win on so many fronts.

I *love her laughter.*

I love the sound, the sight, and the smell of her happiness.

I wish she was happy all the time.

If Luke were here all the time, she'd be happy all the time.

Luke is the best. He brings smiles and cuddles and—

I smell pizza!

Pizza is the best. Luke gives me crusts.

Zella and Luke and pizza are heaven. Every day should be like this.

W ith an open murder investigation, Luke couldn't stay long.

We made an early night of it, but before he left, I did manage to relay my activities of the day, including a CliffsNotes version of the lunch I ended up not sharing with Carson. He didn't even seem particularly bothered by all of my snooping—or he was getting used to it and recognized it as a necessary evil.

The wonderful relaxation brought about by delivery pizza, love shared, and dog cuddles couldn't last forever—but as I closed the door on Luke, I was sad that the moment felt so fleeting.

I allowed myself a few minutes to revel in the cozy feeling of home and belonging, then I pulled out my laptop and got down to business. The first thing I did was check my email to find a few more negative responses to my missing search dog inquiry.

And that was as far as I got on my to-do list.

I had so many complicated feelings wrapped up in resolving the mystery of Fairmont's past. It was a lot to handle on top of Catie's recent murder. So much so that I gave myself a pass on my other laptop tasks for the evening.

A hard pass on replying to emails from my children.

And a strong procrastinate on suspect hunting.

I'd planned to conduct additional research on Catie and Carson (I felt like I was missing something there), to dig through the Cupcakery's social media accounts for anything hateful, and to do a general trawl through the local online paper with particular focus on the editorials and personals looking for anything that might point to another suspect.

Even thinking about what I'd planned for my evening made my head throb. All of which, the delayed research plans and the looming headache, led to the glass of red I'd skipped with the pizza and a very early bedtime for me.

By nine o'clock, I was in bed reading Vanessa and Georgie's latest and curled up with the best dog in the world. No later than ten, Fairmont and I were both dead to the world.

An uncomfortable rumbling pulled me from a deep sleep. My pillow, the one I'd pulled over my head, muffled the noise. But as sleep fell away, I realized it was barking. Loud and persistent barking.

My first uncharitable thought—when would the universe permit me a decent night's sleep? One where I woke of my own volition rather than being dragged from slumber by loud external forces.

And I felt an immediate pang of guilt, because Fairmont only ever barked when there was something to bark about.

That thought pushed away more of my sleep haze and had me almost falling out of bed in my effort to get up quickly.

Fairmont was no longer in bed. He wasn't even in the bedroom.

I hesitated, listening to his barks, trying to pinpoint where in my small house he was, and that was when he yelped.

In pain.

Something, *someone*, had hurt my dog.

Before I could think—thief in the night, armed or not?—I stood in the threshold of my kitchen.

A dark figure in a hoodie lurked in the corner near the back door. It was the sight of him or her that stopped me.

The kitchen was on the opposite side of the house from my bedroom. Faint light from the moon illuminated the scene.

It shone on Fairmont's mostly white coat as he growled, his body stiff and menacing. He stood in the kitchen between me and whoever had broken into my house, apparently unharmed.

Bits of glass littered the floor near my door as proof of the thief's entry point.

Or was this person a thief? Why break into my home with me here? And to steal what? My nonexistent electronics and jewelry?

I recalled the scraps of paper I'd collected over the last several weeks. The ones I'd sealed up tightly in a Ziploc bag, each warning me to leave White Sage and proclaiming me unwelcome in the town. I'd secreted them away, telling no one. Telling myself they meant nothing...and yet clearly they meant something, since I'd kept them.

Maybe my letter writer had decided to do more than write.

I took a step forward, rational thought playing no part in my actions, because I was *angry*. Writing letters. Vaguely threatening me. Tainting the wonderful thing I'd found here in White Sage with nasty notes. Then breaking into my home. Threatening me. Hurting my dog.

"Stop!" a woman yelled, vaguely recognizable. She lifted her hand. A hand that held a very large knife.

Fairmont's growl grew in volume, and the woman's gaze dropped from me to Fairmont.

A woman with a knife now focused all of her attention on my dog. He'd yelped earlier. What had she done to him?

"Fairmont, come." When his head, hunkered low and stretched forward on his neck, didn't turn, I called a second time more urgently.

The growling stopped, and he turned to come stand next to me. I slowly ran my hand along his head, down his back, and along his sides without taking my gaze from the woman standing less than ten feet from me. I couldn't find any sign of injury.

"You..." She lifted the blade, and all I saw was that knife. Everything else fell away.

The tip shook.

I forced myself to follow the tip to the blade to her hand to her body to the face shrouded by a dark hoodie.

"Steph?"

Steph from the Cupcakery?

With a knife. In my kitchen.

This had nothing whatsoever to do with the letters I'd received. This was all about Catie.

"You...with your old lady gossips and your stupid, stupid club." Her hand jerked as if to emphasize exactly how stupid she found it all.

And her voice—something wasn't right with her voice. Something wasn't right with her.

I'd met Steph a few times before. Both before Catie's murder and after. Before Catie died... She'd been the clear-eyed, happy sandy-blonde woman who'd boxed up cupcakes with a smile. She made dog treats that were sold in a handful of shops in town. Turbo and Fairmont loved those treats.

But after Catie's death... I'd felt how fragile she'd been as I'd hugged her. All bones and brittle hair, her eyes red-rimmed. I'd assumed grief. Now I wasn't so sure.

Fairmont pressed his head close to my thigh, grounding me in the here and now.

The here and now, where a woman who was acting unlike herself stood in my kitchen *with a knife*.

A woman who was agitated.

A woman who had broken into my home and thought ahead to bring a *knife* with her.

I really couldn't get away from that knife. Every thought went back to it. For a very good reason. Fairmont and I weren't safe.

Hell. Where was my phone?

Not here, that was where. Not here, nowhere close, and I could kick myself.

Panic settled in, and my chest constricted.

I tried to keep my breaths even—my gut said gasping would agitate the lady with the knife—but it was *hard*. Fairmont pressed his head against my thigh again. I reached down slowly and rubbed his velvet soft ear.

I loved this spotted dog so much.

"Are you crying?" Steph sounded appalled.

"No. Yes." I didn't lift my hand to wipe at the tears, because I didn't want to startle her. She had a *knife*. "You broke into my house. You have a knife. I'm scared."

And angry. Mostly terrified. Also, sad.

An excess of emotion was one way to trigger a crying jag, and I had such an excess rolling through my body that it was a surprise I wasn't curled in the fetal position sobbing. Actually, with Fairmont's help, I was handling this pretty well. I kept rubbing his ear.

"You're scared? You? What about me?"

Much as I would have liked to point out that she was the one with the knife, that didn't seem wise. Silence seemed like the smart alternative. Also, I really needed to find a way to let someone know that everything was not okay.

Or I could just...walk away. Right out the front door. I took a slow step backward.

"No!" Steph screeched as she lunged two steps

forward. "You stay right there. Right there." She stabbed the air with the knife as she spoke.

Looked like I wasn't going anywhere. And now Fairmont was upset from the yelling. He leaned harder against my leg.

"What am I going to do? You... If you hadn't..." She pointed at me with the tip of the blade. "This is all your fault."

Silence was the best option. That was what I'd decided, and yet... "How is it my fault that you murdered Catie?"

Maybe I was stupid like Steph claimed, because if I ever took a hostage negotiation course, I was fairly certain that agitating the person with the weapon would be in the top five things *not* to do. Probably top three.

"Everyone thought she was so wonderful. That Catie was this generous, forgiving person." Steph's face turned ugly. "She wasn't. She fired me! I screwed up once, and she fired me."

Okay... Maybe logic wasn't the way to go, because that came out of nowhere. But she was talking. Maybe she *wanted* to talk about it? Explain herself to someone?

"Please tell me you didn't kill Catie because you lost your job." And maybe I wasn't the right person to get her talking, because I liked Catie. Because I was angry.

Steph lifted the knife and waved it around as she spoke. "What's a job to you? You don't even work. You don't know what it's like to worry where the next meal's coming from."

It was true that I'd been fortunate enough not to fear hunger or homelessness, but if I was understanding what had happened, Catie had given Steph a job. She'd tried to help Steph keep those fears from becoming a reality.

"You...people like you...you don't understand." She was sweating profusely now. She'd inched closer, and I could see that her pupils were huge. "Everyone's against me. The town, your stupid club, you."

This was headed in a very bad direction. The paranoia, the wildly out-of-character aggression, the huge pupils... Drugs?

How was I supposed to reason with a woman whose judgment was impaired by drugs? An armed woman who, while high, still had plenty of motor control to stab me.

She'd stabbed Catie. With this same knife?

"Is this the knife you used to kill Catie?"

She frowned, confused. She looked at the knife in her hand. "No. I didn't have a knife."

I didn't have a knife. She didn't bring one with her?

Maybe she'd used something at the scene. Something from the kitchen. That was where she must have confronted Catie. Then, when the conversation hadn't gone as expected...

But she hadn't brought a knife when she'd attacked Catie. I tried to focus on what that meant in Catie's case, rather than what Steph's choice to bring a weapon to my home meant.

Making my voice as calm and even as I could while my heart raced and my breath puffed from my chest, I said, "You didn't bring a knife when you went to talk to Catie."

She shook her head and her shoulders relaxed— but the knife was still well in front of her body, tip pointed toward me.

"You liked working at the Cupcakery. You just wanted your job back."

She nodded. "When I left work, my hair smelled like sweets. And customers were nice to me at the shop."

My heart twisted in my chest. I didn't know what this woman's life was like outside of her job at Catie's, but if losing a job where people you didn't know smiled back and you came home smelling like sweet treats seemed like the end of the world, then... maybe I didn't want to know.

I didn't want to feel sympathetic. I couldn't. She was a murderer. She'd broken into my home with the intent to harm me.

I channeled that little bit of sympathy that resided in my heart. It was surrounded by fear, but it was there. And I thought it was just enough to make my words genuine. "You didn't mean to hurt her."

Not a question. A statement of fact.

She shook her head again. "I didn't mean to hurt her. I just wanted my job back. I told her I never went to work high. Not one time. But..." Tears and snot started to flow.

"But she knew you were using again."

Steph nodded emphatically but didn't say anything.

"Did she know about the drugs when she gave you the job?"

She used the sleeve of her hoodie to wipe her nose. Her right sleeve, which meant that the knife was pointed away from me and she was distracted for a moment. I inched back, making sure Fairmont stayed at my side.

After she wiped her face, she let her hand fall. With the knife hanging low at her side, I considered making a break for it. But then I recalled her blown pupils. I didn't have experience with people who abused drugs, but I'd seen how erratic her behavior had been thus far. And how quickly she could move.

"When she hired me, she asked. She knew the signs. I guess her cousin or something?"

I nodded, hoping to encourage her to keep

speaking and to find another moment of distraction to increase the distance between us. When she didn't pick up the thread, I said, "You never went to work high...but you started using again?"

Obviously she'd started using again. I couldn't be sure she was high right now. The blown pupils I'd seen earlier could be fear-induced. But her physical appearance had changed significantly in a short period of time, and combined with her erratic behavior, the paranoia...

"When she hired me, she told me no drugs. No drugs, Steph, or I'm going to have to fire you." She looked at me, pleading for understanding. "I never once came to work high. I loved my job."

She really didn't see the issue. And I wasn't about to point it out to her. She was hardly rational. And there was also that knife.

"You didn't mean to kill her," I said, returning to my earlier revelation.

I wasn't placating her. I believed that, unlike tonight, she went to the shop in the early-morning hours to beg Catie to reconsider. But given the time of day, I had to wonder if she'd gone high.

I didn't think Steph went there that night to murder Catie, or even to hurt her. I thought she'd gone there to plead for her job, and then everything went wrong.

She looked at me, and maybe she saw my sincerity. Or maybe she just desperately needed someone, anyone, even the woman she blamed for at least some of her woes, to understand.

She shook her head. "I didn't. I didn't mean to hurt her."

"If you tell Luke that, if you explain—"

"No!" She lifted the knife and shook it in my direction. "I didn't mean to. I didn't. And I'm sorry. I liked Catie, but... I didn't mean to, but..." She stared hard at me. "No one knew. No one would have known. Why did you and your stupid old ladies' club have to get involved? Why?"

She rubbed the side of her head with the palm of her right hand. Like she'd forgotten she was holding a butcher knife in it.

That was when the back door crashed open and into her.

She shrieked.

I yelped.

Fairmont barked.

Amidst the noise and my fear, it took a moment —a long, terrified moment—before I realized the man who'd busted through my back door wore a uniform.

The officer disarmed her immediately, but Steph struggled as he cuffed her.

I watched and wobbled on weak knees, backing away from the flailing banshee she'd become. Backing away from the violence she'd brought into my home. Backing away from the wretched confession she'd made.

I backed right into Luke's waiting arms. I wasn't even surprised to find him behind me. Maybe he'd spoken my name. Or perhaps I'd simply sensed he was there.

He turned me gently to face him, which was when I realized I was clinging to Fairmont's collar. I didn't even remember grabbing it.

Luke gently pried my fingers loose and attached a leash. "I've got him."

I nodded. "There's glass. In the kitchen."

Which was an inane comment. Yes, there was glass. There was also an arrest taking place in my kitchen, and they didn't need Fairmont underfoot.

Luke tugged me gently, his fingers twined with mine, until we were on my front porch. There were several cruisers parked around my house, lights flashing but no sirens.

"Whatever will the neighbors think?" I murmured, proving my sense of humor hadn't completely abandoned me. Then I knelt down to give Fairmont a smothering hug.

Lord love him, he waited quietly, tail wagging, until I finished.

I stood up again and was glad that Luke had hold of Fairmont's leash, because I was feeling a little wobbly. I eyed the pink lounger on my porch, a gift from Luke, and considered if I'd be able to get up if I settled into it. Probably not.

"Do you need a hug?" Luke asked, watching me intently.

I accepted a blanket from another officer with a weak smile. It was the fluffy purple one I kept draped over my sofa. "Definitely, but not right now. I'm sure I'd weep like a terrified, powerless woman whose home has been broken into if you hugged me. I'd prefer not to be that woman for a few more minutes."

"You did really well," he said. "If that helps."

I nodded. It did. "How did you know to come?"

He reached down to pet Fairmont. "The barking. Betsy heard it and was worried, so she wrangled Derek into swinging by to check on you when you didn't answer your phone."

If he'd knocked, neither Steph nor I heard it. I shook my head, not exactly understanding. "I didn't hear him."

"He was a little miffed at his wife for waking him up, and he didn't want to pay that particular favor forward. So in hopes of *not* waking you up, he quietly checked the front door, found it secure, then went around back. He saw the shattered window on the back door. He didn't linger. He withdrew and immediately called the police."

"And went home and hugged his wife, I hope." Thank God for Betsy and her light sleeping.

"No idea, but you can pop around tomorrow." He glanced at his watch. "Well, later today, I suppose, and then you can take care of that yourself. While you're there, give her one from me as well."

I nodded, looking at Luke standing in front of me. Solid, safe, holding Fairmont's leash as if he hadn't anything in the world more important to do. A scan of the area showed no sign of Steph.

Maybe they'd already loaded her up and taken her away.

She'd be going to the same place where the chief had been held. For a little while. Then she'd likely be transferred to the county jail.

Then she'd go to prison.

Suddenly I was so done with it all. Catie's life was gone, Steph's life was ruined, and they'd left a wake of anger and sadness behind them.

I didn't feel an urge to cry or yell or even be held. I was just...numb.

"Fairmont woke you?" Luke asked, taking my elbow and guiding me to his SUV.

"That's right. Though I think it took a little bit. I woke up with my pillow clutched over my head. And then I saw he was gone, not in my bedroom, I mean, and when I went to find him, he was..."

"Right. We heard her confession." After he loaded Fairmont in the back, he settled me into the passenger seat and tucked the blanket closer around me.

"Fairmont growled at her." I shook my head when I realized I wasn't making any sense. "I don't mean tonight. Earlier today."

I thought back to that moment in my car. I'd been parked in front of the Cupcakery and Steph had walked into the store. "He never growls at anyone. I should have known then, but Carson was there and someone else, maybe Angela. So I just didn't think..."

"He could have recognized her scent from the crime scene, but I think it's more likely that he smelled something amiss with her. Drugs change the body's chemistry, and some dogs react poorly— growl or bark—at people who use."

"I didn't know that." I watched the uniformed officers buzzing around my house, feeling detached from it all.

Before Luke closed the door, he leaned close, kissed my forehead, and said, "Give me just a minute. I'll be right back."

He waved a female officer I didn't know over to the SUV. They spoke quietly for a moment, they traded car keys, and Luke disappeared inside my house.

I stared at my sweet little box of a house and silently apologized. I hadn't lost touch with reality. I knew very well that my house had no personality. That it didn't feel the horror of the invasion. That the house hadn't been violated in any way.

But I felt those things, for myself and for the space I'd made my own. A space that was very dear to me.

A few minutes later, Luke returned with a bag. My overnight bag. He loaded it in the back, then opened the passenger door. "Zella, meet Deputy Francetti."

The woman smiled. "Gretchen. Nice to meet you, Ms. Marek."

"Call me Zella, please." Her family name, Francetti, was awfully familiar.

I must have looked confused, because she said, "My cousin is a deputy as well. You met back when Helen was injured."

"That's right. I remember." I looked at the keys in her hand. "I suppose you're driving me to The Hiker this evening?"

She shot a curious look at Luke.

Before she could reply, Luke said, "If you're okay with it, I told Gretchen to drive you back to my place."

I let out a sigh and nodded. I couldn't speak. I was too tired and too relieved. I couldn't handle dealing with anyone right now, and at his house I'd be alone. And I'd feel safe.

"Fairmont can even sleep in the bed." He winked at me.

23

I woke the next morning disoriented by my surroundings and the bright light streaming in the window.

It was October. Such an excess of sunshine indicated an advanced hour, so I must have slept very late indeed.

And then—

I groaned as it all came back to me.

Fairmont shoved his warm body closer to my back, where he'd curled up and slept all night—and morning, apparently. I inhaled deeply, hoping for some trace scent of Luke on the pillow, and I was rewarded with the smell of his laundry detergent and the faintest whiff of his shampoo.

Or maybe I'd imagined it. It didn't matter. I felt

comforted just being in his bed, knowing that was where he laid his head each night.

I could have stayed in the guest room. Possibly what he'd intended when he had Gretchen deliver me here. But this made me happy, and I knew he wouldn't mind. I reached behind me and ran a hand lazily along Fairmont's side. He wouldn't even fuss about the dog hair, because that wasn't the kind of man that Luke was.

The clatter of dishes finally filtered through my sleep-fogged brain, and I realized I wasn't in the house alone.

The noise didn't concern me, because I recognized all the sounds of someone cooking. Since I doubted Luke would be home yet, given the horrendous amount of paperwork he'd be handling today, I could only assume it was Geraldine or the SGG. Maybe both.

I availed myself of the en suite bathroom, one of the advantages Luke's more modern home had over my own. At least if I was facing a horde of curious and potentially cranky old ladies, I'd be doing it after I'd used the restroom, washed my face, and brushed my teeth, and not in the hallway with a full bladder.

And they would be cranky.

The SGG and Geraldine were all overdue a catch-up of my solitary investigations. I should have called a murder meeting after I'd gotten home last night. After I shared everything I'd learned with Luke, there was no reason not to have updated them, other than the fact that I'd been tired. Worn out emotionally more than physically.

I *liked* Catie. I didn't know her terribly well, but she was a woman I would have liked to have known better. That was even clearer to me now, after having poked and prodded into her personal and private life. I sent a silent apology heavenward for the intrusion.

She'd gone to great lengths to keep parts of her life secret. No one but Luke and the chief had known her history with her ex-husband. And still other parts had been if not secret then private. The helping hand she'd given to so many people in the short time she'd been in White Sage, for example.

A rustling noise pulled me into the present. Fairmont's entire head was buried in the bag Luke had so considerately packed for me last night. I had a good idea what he was hunting for.

A few seconds later, he emerged with a Ziploc of his dry dog food clutched in his jaws. Probably best to retrieve it before he punctured holes in the plastic and there was kibble littered throughout Luke's house.

Once I'd safely retrieved the packet of food, I decided it was past time to face the music. I marched into the kitchen to find, as expected, Geraldine and the ladies of the SGG.

I arrived to cheerful greetings. Not a single recrimination. They asked how I'd slept and told me to sit myself down. Which I did after scrounging a bowl for Fairmont's food and depositing his daily ration in it. He had his own water bowl set up permanently in the kitchen, so I didn't have to worry with that.

Georgie delivered a cup of coffee. "It's safe. I brought some of my special beans."

"You're such a coffee snob," I teased her as I accepted the cup with a thankful smile.

Luke's coffee was just fine. I knew for a fact, because I stocked his cupboard with whichever varieties he enjoyed at my house and I only had Georgie-approved coffee.

I clutched the warm mug in my hand. The contents were the perfect shade of dark caramel, because Georgie knew how everyone dear to her took their coffee. I took a sip, pleased to discover she'd found the hemp milk in Luke's fridge.

These ladies were the best. They'd befriended me without hesitation.

White Sage had welcomed me, but Helen, Vanessa, Georgie, and Geraldine had embraced me.

Geraldine seated herself across from me with a

plate of buttered whole wheat toast and black coffee. She didn't say anything, just smiled.

Next was Helen. She brought a plate for me and herself.

Vanessa was next. She brought a plate for herself and Georgie, who followed with their drinks.

Once everyone was seated and, surprisingly, not chatty, I decided it was up to me. I needed to apologize and fill them in.

Before I could voice my regret in not keeping them abreast of developments, Georgie said, "This is an intervention."

She looked at me, eyes wide as she waited for my reaction.

Except... What?

When I didn't reply, she said, "I'm pretty sure we've done this correctly. Vanessa used the Google to research it."

Vanessa nodded. "I did. It seemed wise, given the circumstances."

Geraldine and Helen both murmured their agreement.

I shot a critical glance Helen's way. She seemed a likely source to have inspired this gathering. Interventions seemed right up her alley. She smiled innocently back.

That right there was trouble. Helen was never innocent.

But goodness, an intervention? For what? My first thought was to review my recent eating and exercise habits, one of the areas of my life that could be...fragile, but then I looked down at the plate in front of me, filled with pancakes and a healthy side of bacon.

It didn't seem these ladies were worried about that particular foible, or if they were, they planned to simply stuff me full of carbs and fat whenever our paths crossed.

If not that, then...what?

"You're going to have to be more explicit. I'm not sure what I've done that requires intervention. I haven't started drinking at all hours."

Georgie hummed and looked around guiltily. Just grand. Now I'd have to find out why Georgie had started day drinking.

I continued with a list of other possible issues. "No drugs, no sudden addiction to soaps or reality TV." I'd welcome an intervention on that front. Save me from reality TV.

"That's good to hear," Helen said. We shared an aversion to reality TV.

"Wait, what's wrong with *Dancing with the Stars*?" Vanessa asked.

"And *House Hunters*." Georgie pouted. "I like *House Hunters*."

"And *The Great British Bake-Off*," Vanessa said,

"because technically, that's reality TV. It's relaxing and informative."

"Also *Murder Book*, but I suppose that's mostly research." Georgie frowned. "Yes, I'm calling that research. I don't think I'd like that show if I wasn't taking notes."

Helen sighed. "Forget the reality shows. Stay on topic, ladies." She turned to me. "This is a sleuthing intervention."

"Oh." Suddenly their purpose was clear. I'd fumbled as an SGG member. I'd failed to keep the gang informed, though that didn't explain Geraldine's presence. "I'm sorry I didn't get in touch last night. I planned to update everyone. I promise. I'd have called a murder meeting today once I'd had a decent night's sleep."

I was fairly sure I would have.

"Hmm," Helen said.

And Geraldine leveled me with a critical, mom-worthy stare.

"It's not that you didn't update us," Georgie said, patting my hand. "We think you're taking too many risks."

Since when did sweet, nonconfrontational Georgie become the spokesperson for the SGG and Geraldine?

"I feel responsible," Geraldine said in an uncompromising tone. "I showed up on your doorstep in the wee hours and then practically dragged you to lockup."

I wasn't about to bring up her and "John's" relationship in front of the SGG, but that certainly had been a motivator for her actions. And I really didn't blame her at all. If Luke had been similarly locked up... Well, I'd have done the same as Geraldine, and more.

"And we were busy trying to meet our deadline," Vanessa said.

"Oh, did you finish?" I was excited to read the next book. Also, I didn't like where this conversation was headed.

"Of course we did," Georgie replied sweetly, "thank you for asking." But then she shook her finger at me. Was that glitter in her nail polish? "But that's not the point. We weren't there for you when you needed a keeper."

When *I* needed a keeper? Pot, meet kettle. Georgie and Vanessa and their shady medical records resource. Helen and her head koshing.

"You went off investigating—*alone*—and put yourself in all kinds of danger." Helen leveled that accusation without any hesitation. She was either unaware of the hypocrisy or didn't care.

She was the one who'd gone and gotten her head bashed in by a killer. I just had a knife waved in my face.

And my house broken into.

And I had a terrible suspicion Steph had kicked Fairmont. I hadn't found any shards of glass in his feet, and she hadn't touched him with the knife. Something had made him yelp, and a kick seemed the most likely culprit. Thankfully, he hadn't shown any lasting signs of tenderness last night or this morning.

"I wasn't alone when I had lunch with Heath Carson." It was a weak defense, but also true.

Helen scowled at me. "We'll get back to that Carson man, but what about Miles?"

Georgie swallowed the last bite of her pancake and said, "Oh, Miles is sweet. He wouldn't hurt a fly."

"Exactly," I replied...even though I hadn't known that when I'd let him into my house, and I'd had reservations at the time. "He came by my house. What was I supposed to do? Tell him to wait on the porch while I called backup?"

I was kidding, but leave it to my zany friends to look at each and nod in approval.

"It's unanimous," Vanessa said dryly. "That's a yes."

I would not roll my eyes. After telling Greta it was inappropriate all through her teenage years, I could hardly embrace the response now. So I bit my tongue and waited to see where this intervention was going.

And I also imagined, for just a second, Greta dealing with her own eye-rolling teenage daughter. Much as I'd put my feelings about her recent discovery on hold... I was going to be a grandmother. My daughter was going to be a mother. It was surprising (they hadn't been trying) and wonderful and overwhelming and...so many things that I shouldn't be thinking about in the midst of my "intervention."

"Do you want to tell us why you've become such a risk-taker all of a sudden?" Helen asked. Her sharp gaze felt like it was boring a hole into my very thoughts.

I shelved my thoughts on my approaching grandmotherhood, because, actually, that was a great question.

Yes, I was involved with the SGG primarily to keep an eye on the other members. To keep the ladies out of trouble and well away from harm.

But I was also a part of the SGG because of Fairmont. And because I *hated* unfairness and injustice. Maybe because I'd been cheated on in a marriage that I'd believed was solid. Not at the end, it hadn't been. But the end of my marriage wasn't when the cheating had started. It had started a long, long time ago. When I'd still been fully invested, head over heels, and completely sold on lifetime commitment to one man.

But the why of my participation in the SGG didn't explain my recent change in behavior. Because I had been taking more risks of late.

Four graying heads looked back at me as I processed all of this.

And then words poured out that I didn't plan. Words that reflected feelings I didn't know I had. "You know that my children have been...uncooperative recently. They haven't been supportive, and their lack of support has been on my mind." Four pairs of eyes watched me. "Fine. I'm very annoyed with my children, and I'm not looking forward to the confrontation that's on the horizon. Other, more pressing matters—like this investigation—have let me put my family concerns aside for a little while."

"Are you saying you've been overzealous in your pursuit of a dangerous killer because your children are on your last nerve?" Vanessa asked as if it was something no sane person would do.

And while she might be right, the answer was... "Yes. Or, at least, I think, maybe? And I've also been worried about...other things."

Fairmont's future, keeping three feisty investigators safe from their own sometimes reckless behavior.

At least Geraldine just had a secret romance brewing and not a secret relationship with information dealers on the dark web.

"Hm. You have had a bit more on your plate lately." Helen's gaze slid to Fairmont. She was the only one of the assembled group who was aware of my recent email inquiry.

"I'm not a mother, but..." Georgie looked at me with a frown.

Vanessa picked up where she left off. "But maybe you shouldn't let your kids' bad behavior drive the bus in your relationship. Or let them distract you so much you think it's a good idea to let a strange kid into your house late at night or interrogate an abusive ex-husband."

Georgie shook her head. "I was just thinking that her kids would feel bad if they knew they had anything to do with their mom ending up at knifepoint."

I held up my hand. "I'm not blaming my children. I'm just saying that I haven't been at my best lately, and that maybe I let some personal matters— including but not limited to my children's recent behavior—knock me off my game."

"And?" Geraldine asked with an expectant look.

"And I'll be much more careful." I held up a hand before anyone could celebrate. "*If* you all promise to do the same."

Georgie's sweet expression melted into a scowl. "I'm not giving up Chester."

I looked to Vanessa for clarification. "He's our background check guy," she said.

Before we could delve into the legality of Chester's activities and whether his actions could create legal difficulties for the Crawford sisters-in-law, Helen piped up. "I will make every effort not to be on the receiving end of another concussion."

Geraldine lifted her hands. "Don't look at me. I have enough worries with a son in law enforcement. I'm certainly not looking to take unnecessary risks."

Georgie's pleasant expression had returned as soon as it was clear that no one was going to outright prohibit contact with Chester. "We have some thought on how you can be more careful." She rolled her eyes heavenward. "Though I still don't think sweet Miles was ever any kind of threat."

Ignoring Georgie's comment about Miles, Helen said, "We decided you should get an alarm system."

Her expression dared me to argue.

"I asked Luke about options," Geraldine said. "He said he'd be happy to talk to you about it...if you were interested."

It wasn't a terrible idea, given what had happened.

And that reminder—the reminder of the invasion of my home—brought back my feelings from the night previous. It was as if someone had been through my underwear drawer, as if my privacy had been invaded on a very basic level.

And my small cottage house wasn't exactly the most secure of homes.

Georgie leaned forward, peering at me with a worried expression. "You don't look so good. I'll get you some more coffee."

"And I brought cinnamon buns," Vanessa said, "if you're still hungry."

I smiled weakly. "I'm fine, and no, thank you. I'm full. But I do think an alarm is a good idea. I'll start looking at options." When Geraldine looked disgruntled, I added, "With Luke. I'm sure he can steer me right."

That seemed to mollify her.

"Do you feel properly intervened?" Georgie asked. "We want you to feel safe in White Sage."

"We want her to *be* safe, Georgie," Vanessa said. "Not just feel safe. We don't need a repeat of last night or of that one's concussion." She hitched a thumb in Helen's direction.

"I'll be more careful in the future." With every eye in Luke's kitchen trained on me, I felt compelled to add, "I promise."

A palpable sense of relief washed through the group.

"We thought you'd make more of a fuss." Vanessa squinted. "Plan B was to recruit Luke, but I thought that was going a bit far, especially since you're only a little worse than that one"—she indicated Helen—"and we haven't held an intervention for her or recruited her loved ones to apply pressure."

Only a little worse than Helen?

I really had let my personal life get out of control, if avoiding it had led *me* to becoming the incautious instigator rather than the risk-averse naysayer.

I would be more careful in the future. Updating the SGG along the way. Keeping my phone close by. Installing an alarm at my house.

Also, I would call my children and resolve the issue of their appalling lack of support for my new life and my new love. Having that stressor hanging over my head clearly wasn't in anyone's best interest, since it had negatively impacted my behavior and created stress for my loved ones here in White Sage.

"Now, about this Carson fellow..." Helen stopped when Geraldine rose from the table.

"I have to get back to The Hiker." She paused and gave me a look I couldn't interpret. "I'm also happy to skip this conversation. You let me know how it all works out."

And then she let herself out.

How all *what* worked out?

"How could you let *that man* fund a scholarship

in dear Catie's name? After what he did." Helen shook her head and shot me the look of shame.

But I wasn't about to feel bad. "I don't know how you found out about that."

Helen rolled her eyes. "It's White Sage."

True fact. Gossip was a force all its own, and I had been discussing the idea with Carson in Sally's Sandwich Shop.

"Honestly?" I looked at the faces of the SGG.

Georgie was waiting for my explanation with an open expression. Vanessa looked like she had an opinion, and I might not like it. Helen was upset.

All three waited for me to explain myself.

"First, it was spur of the moment. Second..." I tried to find a way to encapsulate all of the good Catie had done. The way she'd spread hope with the simple act of helping when and where she could. "Miles called himself a White Sage loser."

Georgie made a dismayed sound. "He's such a nice boy. Why would he say that?"

Helen wasn't a native, but Vanessa was, and she understood. "Because he's been pigeonholed as a troublemaking vandal. Graffiti art is a little too avant-garde for this corner of the world, even though it's big business for some artists."

"Everyone knows he's mentoring Matthew?" I asked, hoping I wasn't speaking out of turn. Though it had seemed Miles was more concerned about being caught out for his illegal actions than for his mentoring.

"No." Vanessa appeared intrigued by the idea. "Good for him, and I'll keep that one under my hat."

"When he came to the house, he said he and Angela were White Sage losers, like the town had given up on them. Catie didn't. And she helped Liam with his college application. She gave Steph a job when she desperately needed not only to the pay the bills, but also something to be proud of."

"*That* didn't turn out so well." Helen's caustic tone grated on my frazzled nerves.

"No, Helen, it didn't. But that's not the point. The point is that it was Catie's choice to help her. Catie chose to help people, to give a second chance where she could. And this money, wherever it's coming from, will be used to do the same."

"It won't have his name. It will have hers." Georgie leaned forward. "I say take the money and run. Keep Catie's name alive by helping to lift up others."

"I think we should get locals to contribute," Vanessa said. "We have some folks in the area who could be talked into helping. It is a good cause. And that way, we make it ours."

Helen sighed. "it would be good to get more kids into college without racking up debt."

"Kids who might not be able to go otherwise," I added.

"Okay, fine. I see your point," Helen said. "But I don't have to like that the money—sorry, Vanessa, I do think you're right about local contributions—that *some* of the money will come from that man."

And the reason I'd bothered to convince these three highly motivated, energetic women that the scholarship was a good idea no matter how it was funded, was because I wanted them to help me create it.

By the time they left, I was sure enough of their commitment to contact my accountant. She agreed to reach out to Carson with a proposal, one that would keep him well away from any administering, that would make him an anonymous donor only.

The town would embrace a scholarship honoring Catie and spearheaded by the SGG. I was sure of it.

And after speaking with my accountant, I picked up the phone to call my daughter.

I might have had a glass of Luke's good whisky first, but that was between me and the whisky bottle.

24

A few days later, I was sitting on the sofa in my own home. My back door had been repaired, and I'd even hosted a breakfast in the kitchen with the SGG in hopes of erasing any lingering feelings of unease associated with the room.

I had at least three days of guilt-free reading and lounging planned. After facing a knife-wielding lunatic, I figured I deserved it.

I'd already taken Fairmont on a run and then followed that up with a bubble bath. Couch surfing with Vanessa and Georgie's latest was the last on my list of decompression tasks for the day. I only had a few chapters left and I was eager to read them, especially since they'd finished up the next in the series and it was due to release soon.

I was just picking up my e-reader when my phone rang.

I didn't recognize the number, and it wasn't programmed in my contacts.

I answered with a polite, but not particularly warm, greeting.

"Hi," a woman tentatively said. "Is this Zella Marek?"

"Yes, this is Zella."

Almost all of the calls I received were from numbers programmed in my contact list. Since this one wasn't, and I wasn't expecting a call from anyone in particular, I did that reflexive scan that I'm sure many mothers of grown children must do in similar situations: where would Greta or Mark still have me listed as an emergency contact? And what situation would result in an emergency call? Did this have something to do with Greta's pregnancy?

Before I could travel down that treacherous path, the caller identified herself. "I'm Sarah Wilson. You don't know me, but, ah, I think you may have adopted my husband's dog."

My heart raced in my chest. I would not cry. I would make my case, hear hers, and evaluate the situation. I would make certain that Fairmont's best interests were kept in mind at all times.

Why was she calling? I would so much rather do this by email, where perspective would be easier to maintain. How did she even get my number? I didn't include it in my email.

But I didn't ask those questions. That would have been too difficult, given the massive lump that had lodged somewhere between my heart and my mouth. I cleared my throat. "Oh?"

"Yes. One of his old team members reached out to me. He knew Silas had gone missing during a very difficult time, and I guess the timeline added up. He figured there couldn't be that many missing search dogs, so he reached out to me when he got your email."

"Silas?" I croaked.

Fairmont's head popped from the opposite end of the sofa. His ears perked, and he gave me a curious look. Oh, no.

"Liver and white ticked German shorthaired pointer. I'd have to look at his papers, but about five? Maybe six years old."

I cleared my throat again. "Yes. That sounds like the dog I adopted from the shelter."

"We can come pick him up, if that's what you want." Again, she sounded tentative.

"Maybe we can talk about that?" I asked, equally as uncertain. I didn't want Fairmont picked up, but why was she calling me and offering to come get him if that wasn't what she wanted?

She let out a loud breath. "Look, I'm going to

level with you. I hunted up your phone number because I didn't want there to be any confusion when we discussed this. We will absolutely take him back. He's welcome here. He'll have a home with us forever if that's what needs to happen, but I thought maybe..."

My heart thudded erratically as Fairmont watched from his dog bed. He must have sensed something was wrong, because he crawled the length of the sofa and replanted himself next to me.

"I'd very much like to keep him. He's so happy here, and I—"

"Oh, thank goodness." Sarah laughed. "You have no idea how happy I am to hear that."

I was so confused. "But—"

"Honey, when you reached out looking for his home, I assumed you'd adopted him and figured out he was too much for you. That you were doing your due diligence before placing him with a rescue or looking for a home for him yourself."

"No! I adore Fairmont."

His head popped up again, and this time his little stubby tail wagged.

The grin on my face was practically making my cheeks hurt. "I couldn't imagine finding a more amazing dog."

Silence greeted my statement.

"Hello?"

"I'm still here." Sarah chuckled. "I'm just...well, surprised. He's a fireball. A great search dog, from what my husband used to tell me, but just a lot of dog to handle for someone who wasn't used to working dogs."

I blinked at the dog who was now dead-bugged on my couch, his feet sticking up in the air. His head flopped back so that his nose rested on my thigh. His canines flashed in the least menacing way possible as his lips drooped with gravity. He was so adorable like this. Most certainly *not* a fireball.

"Um, maybe we're not talking about the same dog." Except I knew we were. "He's such a gentleman. Can you hold on for a second?"

When she agreed, I took a quick picture and texted it to her.

She was laughing by the time I picked the call up again. "Same dog, and yet very, very different. Zella, can I ask why you reached out? You obviously care for him, and you had to know there'd be a possibility that his previous owners would want him back."

"I moved recently, and..." How did I explain this? Probably short and sweet was best. "I don't know how else to say this. There was a dead body in my backyard."

Sarah's laughter bubbled up and overflowed. She gasped and stopped. "Oh, gosh. I'm so, so sorry. I shouldn't laugh. That must have been terrible for you. But wow, that must have been a sight."

"It was upsetting, but I get exactly what you mean. What are the chances? And it was certainly a sight. Fairmont was amazing. He actually might have saved my friend's life. Not long after that, he followed a blood trail to find her."

Sarah took a deep breath. Her voice wavered when she spoke, and I didn't think it was with laughter. "My husband will be so thrilled that Silas was able to help you find your friend."

Each time she mentioned her husband, my unease grew. "My boyfriend is the local sheriff, and he explained to me how much training was required to train a cadaver dog. He thought maybe Fairmont, Silas, might have had some trailing training as well?"

"Yes, he's cross-trained in both disciplines, but most of his deployments were as a cadaver dog. And you probably wouldn't believe the amount of training unless you actually saw it. It's very time-consuming." She didn't sound too pleased about it, and I didn't know what that meant.

"It's because of all the training that I reached out to the local search groups. I thought there might be someone out there missing him. Worried about him." I hated to ask. Everything was going so well. I couldn't ask for a better outcome, and yet several of her comments made me uneasy. "Do you need to speak to your husband? It sounds like Fairmont, Silas, was his dog. And all of the training he did with him, well, maybe you need to speak to him?"

"No. No, I don't need to speak with him. He'll be so pleased to hear how this has all turned out. That Silas has found a home where he's so loved. He'll adore the picture." She paused. "My husband doesn't do search and rescue any longer. He had a stroke. That's why I called. Speaking on the phone is still very difficult for him."

"I'm so sorry to hear that." Fairmont's cold nose touched my hand, and I reached down to rub his exposed belly.

Voice firm and filled with a forced cheer with which I was intimately acquainted, she said, "He's doing very well, better than expected. But he doesn't expect to be in the field again as a canine handler. We discussed possibly finding a SAR home for Silas if he came back, but this is so much better."

"He has been such a comfort to me. He's an amazing dog." I rubbed his stomach again. "He has his very own fan club here in White Sage."

"Does he? That's so wonderful." I could hear the smile in her voice. After a short pause, she said, "You said before, about someone worrying about him... It was my fault that he got loose. I was so over-whelmed. It was days after Bill's stroke, and taking care of the dogs wasn't my highest priority at the time. We both thought, well, we thought he'd been killed by coyotes or hit by a car. I checked the local shelter, informed the local vets. And he's chipped, so we thought if he'd gone through any shelter system that they'd have contacted us."

"Oh, they checked for a chip." I knew they did, because the process had been explained to me when I adopted Fairmont. "Both when he was brought in and before they chipped him as a part of the adoption process. I guess it malfunctioned?"

"I don't know, and I guess at this point it doesn't matter. I'm just so relieved that he's alive and so well taken care of." She sniffed. "So, just to reiterate. *Fairmont* always has a home here if he needs one, but I'm so, so happy that he's found someone new to love."

We ended the call with an exchange of information. She wanted my mailing address to send transfer of ownership paperwork for Fairmont, and I asked if I might make a donation in Fairmont's honor to the local search group or if there was another place they'd prefer.

And that was that. Fairmont was well and truly mine.

My heart had never doubted he belonged here, with me, in my home. But my conscience would have weighed heavily if I hadn't reached out and at least tried to find the people who had invested so much of their time in him.

Thank goodness I did. Now his former owners could put their minds at rest, knowing that while he may have had a rough transition, Fairmont had settled into a home where he was loved.

It wasn't until about a week later, when I received a letter from Bill and Sarah, that I realized I still had concerns.

Would Bill change his mind?

Would he want Fairmont back as a pet? It wasn't as if my spotted buddy was training or working in my home. He was a couch potato about ninety percent of the time. The other ten, he was jogging with me or chasing squirrels in the backyard.

Maybe Sarah had oversold her husband's comfort level with Fairmont remaining in my care.

I opened the letter to find a packet of papers from Fairmont's breed registry. Attached with a paper clip were instructions from Sarah for completing the transfer.

But there was a second note. One from Bill.

It wasn't long, and it was clear from the awkward shape of the letters and the unintentional squiggles that the few written words on the page hadn't come easily to him. The obvious effort made his words that much more meaningful.

Basically, he thanked me. For loving his dog. For the pictures. (I'd sent a few more dignified versions that I'd captured over the last week.) For sharing

Fairmont's story of saving Helen from an unknown fate in the hands of a killer.

He wrote that he'd been a cadaver handler for twenty years. Trailing was new. It made him so proud that a dog he'd trained had helped save someone's life.

And that was it.

He expressed no doubts, and he wished the two of us health and happiness.

After reading his letter, I desperately needed to hug *my* dog.

"Fairmont, come!"

25

I hear my lady calling.

I run to her side and she wraps her arms around me.

My lady gives the best hugs.

She tells me she loves me and hugs me and hugs me.

I love her so much.

I hope she knows.

I tell her in all the ways I know.

I sleep in her spot on the sofa when she's away, so she comes home and it's warm for her.

I trot so very slowly so I don't pull on the leash when she takes me for a "run."

I always (sometimes) wait patiently for her to make coffee before she feeds me in the morning.

I cuddle close to her at night when she's worried, so she knows in her sleep that she's safe.

And I share Luke with her without complaining, because Luke makes her as happy as he makes me.

FAIRMONT-APPROVED DOG TRAINING TIPS

3 Ways to Win Treats & Cuddles (Fairmont)

1. Lie quietly and unobtrusively under the kitchen table when guests are invited for meals. They'll either forget you're there, so you win all the dropped pieces of food. Or they'll be so impressed by your polished manners that they share their meal.

2. Keep all the best spots warm for your favorite human: Zella's spot on the sofa, her side of the bed, the driver's seat of the car. When your human returns, pretend to be snoozing, and you'll be "woken" with all the best pets.

3. Pretend you don't hear your person

calling when the fluffy tails of squirrels are waved in your face, and then, on the third or fourth try (after the fluffy squirrel butts have departed), "hear" the call and immediately bound toward your person as fast as you possibly can. Your enthusiasm will be rewarded! Who would ever hold you responsible for the commands you failed to hear?

3 Ways to Encourage Gentlemanly Behavior (Zella)

1. Remember to promptly and consistently reward good behavior. It's often less noticeable than naughty behavior, so I have to remind myself. Pets, verbal praise, and treats work well. For example, I reward Fairmont for being on his best behavior when the SGG comes over for murder meetings or even just for a chat. If he lies quietly under the table or on his dog bed, he gets little treats through the meeting.

2. Whenever your pooch usurps your spot for naps, wake him with sweets pets, then nudge him to a new spot. Unless...he's really sleepy, then maybe cuddle next to him instead.

3. Always reward your pooch when they come, even if it's not right away because your dog is being teased by rodent devils, aka squirrels. And maybe consider squirrel deterrents for the yard. And a dog training consult.

TRACKING A POISON PEN, FAIRMONT
AND ZELLA'S NEXT MYSTERY!

Nasty notes and deadly deeds

Zella's had enough of the horrid letters she's been receiving since she moved to White Sage. Scrawled on scraps of paper and left near her home to find, each of the notes shares the same theme: go home.

Except...White Sage *is* Zella's home. No one is making her feel unwelcome in her adopted town.

She enlists the Sleuthing Granny Gang to help her track down the poison pen letter writer...and that's when the first body appears.

Join Zella, Fairmont, and the rest of the Sleuthing Granny Gang in their latest adventure!

Tracking a Poison Pen *is available for preorder now.*

Keep reading for an excerpt from Cate's paranormal cozy mystery series Vegan Vamp Mysteries.

**EXCERPT: ADVENTURES OF A
VEGAN VAMP**

PROLOGUE

I died a little.

I wish I could say it was a blur, but it's a blank. A mystery.

I was an anxiety-ridden, overachieving, successful (and perhaps not entirely likable) professional—and human. I definitely started this story very human.

But now I'm none of those things.

This story is about the murder of that woman and catching the man who killed her. It's also about how I became a vampire and also a little about how becoming a vampire was the best thing that could have happened to me.

CHAPTER: The Flu

Why did my mouth feel like it had been stuffed with cotton balls? I tried to swallow and almost threw up in my mouth.

Not good. Very not good. I held my breath and fought the urge to swallow again.

I needed to be absolutely still. Moving made me want to ralph, and I would never make it to the bathroom.

Even the thought of moving made my head pound with a vicious rhythm.

My eyelid cracked of its own volition and the pain at the base of my skull and behind my eyes ratcheted up. I carefully shut my eyes and lay very, very still.

Finally, after counting backward from a hundred, I started to feel myself drift away.

***

A desert surrounded me. A cool desert. A cool, dry desert.

Slowly, I became aware of the feel of the sheets against my skin, the pillow under my head. And then the parched, cottony feel of my mouth.

I almost groaned—almost—but then I remembered the gut-piercing, brain-pounding pain from earlier. The feeling that my head would explode into a billion tiny pieces. So I didn't make a sound.

Time passed. A little? A lot? I lay in my bed—still, in pain, and afraid—for I don't know how long...but then I realized I was thirsty. Wandering-the-desert, no-water-for-days thirsty.

I opened my mouth a little and experimented with moving my lips. The pulling sensation that forewarned of cracking skin stopped me.

Water had *never* sounded so glorious. I could feel it slipping past my lips, moistening my mouth... And then I did groan, because there was no water.

And my head exploded in pain, followed by a black nothingness.

***

Someone had superglued my eyelids shut. Somewhere in the back of my brain, I realized that was B.A.D. Kidnapping, home invasion, a *Criminal Minds*-type serial killer—scenarios flashed through my mind.

But I wasn't afraid. I experienced, in fact, a complete absence of fear. I was simply too tired to feel any strong emotion.

I must have drifted off to sleep again, because when I woke up I vaguely remembered thoughts of superglue and kidnapping, but this time I realized how insane that was, mostly because I could open my eyes—just.

It took some delicate prying, but I managed to

eventually see the light of day. I'd had allergy attacks that left my eyes crunchy—I lived in allergy central, a.k.a. Austin, Texas—but the crud in my eyes was something entirely different.

Whatever the funky goo was, the effort of unsticking my eyelashes from it had wiped me out. I lay on my bed and tried to summon up sufficient energy to move, but it wasn't happening.

Lying there with my mind awake and my body incapacitated, I couldn't help but dwell on my drier-than-dirt mouth. I tried to lick my lips, but it didn't help.

I needed a drink. *Water.* I almost shivered, I was so excited. The thought of water was finally enough to make me think about getting up.

At least the gnarly headache that I'd been sporting the last time I woke up was gone. But I had crystal-clear memories of that pain, and it was those memories that made me cautious. I slowly rolled onto my side. My muscles protested. The deep muscle aches made me wonder if I'd come down with the flu.

Headache, nausea, aching muscles—I stopped inventorying my symptoms and lifted the back of my hand to my forehead and then my cheek. Dry and cool to the touch; no fever. A feverless flu? I also had the oddest feeling that I hadn't moved since I'd fallen asleep. And I *never* slept on my back; I was a side sleeper.

Flu or no flu, that water wasn't getting any closer. In one quick motion, I rolled off my bed and onto my feet—and promptly collapsed in a heap on the floor.

Abstract thoughts of superglued eyes and kidnapping hadn't done it, but now I was worried. I needed a drink. How long had I been asleep? And I still didn't feel like I needed to pee. I *always* had to pee as soon as I woke up. I had to be dangerously dehydrated.

Where was my phone? I usually left it plugged in next to my bed, and it was hard to believe I'd slept through my alarm. Mustering up enough energy to crawl, I inched my way to the bedside table where my phone was plugged in. With what seemed a monumental effort, I grabbed the phone. I propped myself up against my bed and tapped the screen.

Nuts. Fourteen missed calls, twenty texts… how…? It was late and I'd missed work, but fourteen missed calls. A nasty feeling washed over me. The wallpaper on my phone had a large digital clock that read nine fifty-three—but there was no date. I flicked the screen down. My eyes didn't want to focus. Or my mind was playing tricks. Friday the twentieth. That simply wasn't possible; I'd gone for happy hour drinks on Tuesday. I couldn't have been in bed for three days. Someone would have checked on me... wouldn't they?

After dialing voicemail, I tapped the speaker button and then started to scroll through my texts. After five minutes it was clear: no one had thought to check on me. I'd been berated for not calling in, for missing appointments, and for failing to attend meetings. By my boss and my coworkers. By voicemail and text. I'd made a mistake, and they'd reveled in it.

The effort of retrieving my phone had so depleted my strength that I couldn't do more than lie on the floor. So I curled up and wallowed in self-pity.

To be so alone that no one suspected I was unwell or injured after I'd been missing for three days? Miserable. Pathetic. A desolate existence. I realized as I cried that no tears fell.

I hacked out dry sobs that burned my throat, because I'd never made it to the bathroom for that drink of water.

CHAPTER: How Am I alive?

I was broken.

Something was wrong with me, with my body, and I had two days to find out what it was. Two days, and even then I'd probably be begging to keep my job, if those texts and voicemails were any indication. I needed to sort out what was happening to me, and I also needed some kind of believable excuse explaining away my three days off the grid.

Last night I'd eventually managed to make it to the bathroom, consume an unbelievable quantity of water, and fall asleep again. Here it was, ten a.m. on Saturday, and I still hadn't peed. What person goes four days without peeing?

After trawling the internet, I discovered people did go four days and even longer without urinating, but none of the scenarios I'd found seemed likely to apply to me. Thank you, Google.

Going to the doctor seemed wise, imperative even...except for the part where I had to get out of bed, get dressed, and actually get there. I rolled over in bed. Then I rolled again and sat up. The soreness was gone. I was exhausted, yes, but the deep muscle aches had vanished.

Tired I could manage. I'd pulled a few all-nighters in business school and knew some tricks. Group projects still left a nasty taste in my mouth. There was always one underachiever who didn't do their part, and never in a predictable, manageable way. Experience taught me that I could push through exhaustion with determination (which I had in spades), caffeine (which waited in the kitchen), and a shower (which sounded delightful).

After I'd put the kettle on to boil and ground some fresh beans, I sat down with my laptop at the kitchen table. I drafted a quick note to my boss that I'd come down with a terrible flu, hadn't left my bed in days, and would be back to work on Monday. I groveled as best I could, reread it to make sure I sounded sincerely apologetic without tumbling into desperation, and then clicked send.

It all sounded reasonable enough but for one small detail: my boss had actually met me. Anyone that had spent more than a few minutes with me would know that I'd call in in between puking bouts. The only thing that could keep me from calling in was a coma. Or death. The piercing whistle of the kettle distracted me from pursuing that morbid thought.

Five minutes later, I marched into my bathroom with my French-pressed coffee in hand, ready to tick off the next item on my list. A shower should be a nice pick-me-up. Although—oddly enough—I didn't feel like I'd spent the last four days sick in bed. And I hadn't noticed any weird odors.

If you didn't shower for four days, you smelled. A simple fact of life every woman past puberty understands. But what would I tell my doctor? I'm fresh as a daisy even when I don't shower—isn't that weird? I shook my head and turned to flip the water on.

Hot coffee splashed my thighs as my mug fell from nerveless fingers, and the sound of shattering ceramic echoed in my ears as if from a great distance.

The gaunt-faced image across from me jumped, and I yelped in surprise.

Her mouth moved as if yelping in surprise.

I took a cautious step away from her...and she did the same in reverse.

"Oh, no. Nononono." I lifted my hand to my shockingly thin face. "No."

My knees ceased supporting my weight, and I sank down to perch on the lip of the tub. And for the first time since I'd gained consciousness the previous evening, I looked closely at my hands. Long, elegant fingers. Too thin to be my fingers. I inspected my right hand and found no age spot just below the knuckle of my index finger. No blemishes at all. The fine lines that had become invisible to me over the last few years were marked now by their absence.

My forearms had become a series of interconnected freckles more years ago than I could remember. Since my mid-twenties, maybe? A light, even tan now covered my forearms.

I dropped my head into my hands, but that was a mistake. My own flesh felt alien. My face had once had a pleasant roundness to it that I'd become accustomed to. The new sharpness of my chin and the definition of my cheekbones felt foreign under my fingertips.

Inhale, two, three. Exhale, two, three. Inhale, two, three. Exhale, two, three.

That therapist had been good for something after all, because when I opened my eyes I had a plan.

To keep reading, download your copy of *Adventures of a Vegan Vamp* now!

AUTHOR'S NOTE

If you read the second Fairmont Finds book, then you've already met Turbo. He makes a slightly more substantial appearance in book 3, because he's too cute not to be a regular character!

Just a reminder, Turbo is based on a real German shorthaired pointer, adopted from Texas German Shorthaired Pointer Rescue.

Turbo, full name Turbo Klaus, was adopted by the Sauter family, and they couldn't be happier to have him join their family. Thank you again, Sauter Family, for your contributions to TGSPR and for providing a home for this rambunctious angel.

ABOUT THE AUTHOR

When Cate's not tapping away at her keyboard or in deep contemplation of her next fanciful writing project, she's sweeping up hairy dust bunnies and watching British mysteries.

Cate is from Austin, Texas (where many of her stories take place) but has recently migrated north to Boise, Idaho, where soup season (her favorite time of year) lasts more than two weeks.

She's worked as an attorney, a dog trainer, and in various other positions, but writer is the hands-down winner. She's thankful readers keep reading, so she can keep writing!

For bonus materials and updates, visit her website to join her mailing list: www.CateLawley.com.

Made in the USA
Las Vegas, NV
28 April 2021